THE NOT SO NICE LIST

SALLY KILPATRICK

What folks are saying about
Sally Kilpatrick's novels...

...for *The Happy Hour Choir*
"Kilpatrick mixes loss and devastation with hope and a little bit of Southern charm. She will leave the reader laughing through tears. This is an incredible start from a promising storyteller." –*RT Book Reviews*
"Witty, warm, and as complex and heart-wrenching as only love and family can be." –*Heroes and Heartbreakers*

...for *Bittersweet Creek*
"Pleasantly engaging." –*Library Journal*
"Fans of Southern contemporary romance will be charmed." –*Publisher's Weekly*

...for *Better Get to Livin'*
"Sweet, funny, and charming…. Absolutely Lovely." –*Bookish Devices*
"In short, this one is pretty much as close to perfect as a reading experience can get." –*Nashville Book Worm*
"Readers will both laugh and cry as Declan and Presley face loss, learn life lessons from ghosts, and realize life is much easier to handle with someone by your side." –*Booklist*

"Don't miss this quirky, fun love story. I couldn't put it down." –
Haywood Smith, *New York Times* Bestselling author
"Kilpatrick and her signature quirky characters are back! This is a
fun story about following your heart even through life's unexpected detours and not letting fear hold you back. Some familiar
characters combine with new ones, great visuals, even some
ghosts. The reader may notice some hints of *It's a Wonderful Life*
woven in. They may also wish they had an Uncle Hollis—
complete with Elton John obsession—in their own family." –*RT
Book Reviews*

…for *Bless Her Heart*
"With both humor and insight, Bless Her Heart hits all the right
notes in the complicated song of becoming who we are meant to
be. This novel asks us to look at the "rules" we might just have to
break to heal our own life. Do yourself a favor and grab this book
and hide away with its laugh-out-loud and cry-out-loud moments
all mixed up in one place. Kilpatrick enthralls us again with her
trademark quirky humor and vivid characters." –Patti Callahan
Henry, *New York Times* bestselling author
"I rank *Bless Her Heart* right up there with *The Happy Hour Choir*. It
is a little bit Flannery O'Connor, a little bit Fannie Flagg, but most
delightfully and originally Sally Kilpatrick. –*The Romance Dish*
"Anybody from the South knows that 'Bless her heart' is one of
those phrases that sounds sweet but actually is code for the worst
kind of holier-than-thou, southern-fried judgment. In much the
same way, Sally Kilpatrick's touching new novel *Bless Her Heart* is
a light smooth read on the surface but has plenty of bite under-
neath." –Kim Wright, author of *Last Ride to Graceland*

…for *Oh My Stars*
"Kilpatrick creates a charming town full of lovable oddballs in the
story of Ivy, Gabe, and their extended families, making this a yule-
tide treat that will warm readers' hearts." –*Library Journal*
"Captures all of the sweet and sassy of a cozy Southern town…

Takes the story beyond a romance to a novel about self-discovery. Fans of fun Southern towns [and] Christmas miracles will rejoice." –*Booklist*

"*Oh My Stars* hits all the right emotional beats. If you can walk away from this book without getting a bit of a lump in your throat or misty eyes, then you are a better reader than I am." –*The Nashville Book Worm*

"This is a really sweet holiday themed romance everyone can enjoy." –*Harlequin Junkie*

…for *Much Ado about Barbecue*

"Sally Kilpatrick's blend of tender love, bruised memories, and fragrant slow-cooked pork is the perfect antidote to the woes of the world….Delicious in every way." –Emily Carpenter, bestselling author of *Burying the Honeysuckle Girls*

"Sally Kilpatrick returns with her signature Southern charm and humor in this enchanting romance that will make you hunger for more (pun intended)" –Jamie Beck, *WSJ* and *USA Today* bestselling author

"Classic Kilpatrick" –Liz Talley, author of *Deconstructed*

"Kilpatrick serves up some whole-hog barbecue and a helluva romance….she proves she's a pitmaster of love and laughs." Ken Wheaton, author of *Duck Duck Gator*

For Ryan, my preeminent scholar on Christmas movies

Aubrey

It was weird and more than a little creepy for a twenty-eight-year-old woman to be sitting in Santa's lap, but that's exactly where I found myself. In all fairness, the photo shoot hadn't been my idea. Isaac, my boss, wanted some photos for a calendar he was sending as a Christmas present from the liquor distributor where we worked. No doubt he considered me a cheap model substitute since I worked as his secretary.

He also wanted to get into my pants because he was a sexist pig. Why was I still at this job? Why was I even here at a mall before opening hours? Because I was going to hold down a job for at least six months or die trying.

I pasted on a smile and hoped I wasn't showing too much leg next to the bottle of high-end tequila perched on my hip. I had no idea where Isaac had found this Mrs. Claus get up, and I was afraid to ask.

Ah, the things I did for my job.

I couldn't afford to lose this one because I already had an impressive string of failed careers and failed relationships behind me. Waitress? Dumped tray of spaghetti on a mayoral candidate. Retail? Accidentally gave back change for a hundred instead of a ten. Babysitter? Kid set the house on fire while I ran to the bathroom for just a second.

Santa, I could tell, was not amused by my latest stop on the job train, and there was no telling what lie Isaac told the mall to make this photo shoot happen. At least we were taking these pictures before the mall opened so none of the kids would witness it.

"Hold on, let me take a look at these," Isaac said as he looked down at his expensive camera. A short, wizened woman in a green elf costume stood beside him, tapping her foot. With her arms crossed over her chest and a scowl on her face, it was clear she wasn't happy about the proceedings, either.

I caught movement in the corner of my eye and saw my housemate, Cole Frost, gawking.

What the heck is he doing here?

He never took a day off. He didn't believe in mental health days or spontaneity or...fun. It would be my luck that he would witness yet another lapse in my judgment.

My skin prickled at the thought of his disapproval. And to think I'd had a crush on him all through high school because I thought the glasses made him hot in a nerdy, intense sort of way.

That was before he moved in and started berating me about dishes in the sink and where I left my socks. No doubt he would tell my brother about the whole thing, them being tight and all, and then the whole family would make fun of Aubrey over Christmas dinner.

It could be my gift to them since making fun of me was a favorite pastime for the whole family—minus me, of course.

"Ho, ho, ho," said the snowy bearded man in whose lap I sat. "While we wait, I might as well ask. What's your name, little girl?"

It was on the tip of my tongue to say something sarcastic, but the twinkle in his eyes stopped me. There was something about him that just *felt* sincere. Even more importantly, he'd been very careful *not* to cop a feel. And his beard? Definitely real.

"Aubrey. Aubrey Longfellow."

"Why, that sounds like an elf's name."

"Aubrey does mean 'elf ruler.'" I smiled in spite of myself.

"And the Longfellows are a very good family, even if they should probably be called the short fellows," he said with a wink.

I grinned, utterly charmed in spite of myself. Who knew where the mall had found this guy, but he was the real deal. Parents were going to bring their kids from all over to meet him.

"And what would you like for Christmas?" Santa asked in a tone of voice that didn't hold an ounce of double-entendre. This man was kind and genuine. Something about him made me want to ask for a kitten or a bicycle or that Nintendo Wii I never got even though I was an absolute angel that year.

Well, almost an angel.

I shifted a little and opened my mouth to tell him about the Wii.

"For God's sake, Aubrey, I can see your underwear." Cole's voice carried across the mall.

I jumped out of Santa's lap and started adjusting my skirt. My face burned. Why did it have to be Cole who saw me?

Shame melted into anger. How was it any of his business how I was dressed?

I flipped him off, in front of Santa and everyone.

Cole threw his hands up in the air, shaking his head in a combination of disgust and defeat before walking away. Now I felt bad for flipping him off.

No, he shouldn't have yelled at me across the mall.

"Know what I want for Christmas?" I turned to Santa. "I'd like for Cole Frost to get that stick out of his butt, get out of my business, and get out of my house."

Santa gasped, his eyes growing wide. Then he sighed deeply. "I wish you hadn't said and done that, Aubrey."

"Why?" I smoothed my skirt. The elf beside Isaac had turned her glare on me now. "He is such a pain in my…posterior. It would only be fair if he left me alone."

He shook his head. "I can't speak to what's fair, but now you're on the Not So Nice List."

The what?

This guy was taking the Santa thing too far. "There's no such thing as a Not So Nice list. Nor a Naughty List. And if there were, Cole Frost would be at the top of it."

"Oh, there's very much a Naughty List, and now you're close to being on it. The Not So Nice List is for boys and girls who've been very, very good all year, only to have a lapse in judgment in December."

I crossed my arms over my chest and tilted my head to the side in what Mom used to call my sassy look. Nothing like visiting Santa to make me regress, I guess. "So what? I wasn't going to get anything for Christmas anyway."

Santa sighed and shook his head. "Oh, Aubrey. Just because you had one bad Christmas back in 2006 doesn't mean that the Naughty List—or the Not So Nice List—isn't a thing."

"Wait. How…?"

"It wasn't *my* fault you didn't get that Wii, I'll have you know. But being on the Not So Nice List is about more than getting passed over for toys. You see, naughty begets naughty, so it's kinda like, well, being on the Not So Nice List is a lot like always having Mercury in retrograde—especially for adults. If you're on the Not So Nice List, nothing is going to go right for you for an entire year."

"Oh, for crying out loud." I rolled my eyes so far into the back of my head I could almost see the Starbucks kiosk behind me. "I don't believe in astrology or luck, and I don't believe in Santa either."

It was his turn to tilt his head to the side and study me with a stern look. "You don't mean that, Aubrey."

"I totally do."

"So you didn't check your horoscope this morning?"

I opened my mouth to reply, but I wasn't about to lie to Santa. "Fine. I did read my horoscope. But how did you…?"

His eyes twinkled.

More than a little weirded out, I backed up one step, then two, and then tripped over a cord to the photography lights and fell flat on my ass.

Isaac laughed out loud, the sound echoing around the blessedly empty mall. I looked to see if Cole might have returned to the little white picket fence that cordoned off Santa's Wonderland. He wasn't there. I couldn't tell if I was relieved or disappointed. At least he wouldn't have laughed at me.

Santa got up with a grunt and waddled over to offer me a hand. He lifted an eyebrow as if to say, "See?"

"This is ridiculous," I muttered under my breath, but I took his hand and let him pull me to my feet. Digging deep for my manners, I said, "Well, thank you for the photo shoot, Mister...?"

"Kringle. Kris Kringle."

"Right." I jabbed a thumb over my shoulder in the direction of my boss. "Is *he* on the Naughty List?"

Santa sighed. "I don't think he's ever left it."

Well, that might be an argument for the existence of such a list.

I nodded and went on my not so merry way. I'd driven myself so I wouldn't have to be in close quarters with Isaac. If I hurried I could have a few minutes of peace after my drive back to work.

As I'd hoped, I beat Isaac back to the office. He'd gone to Starbucks without even asking me if I'd like something. Mind you, if I did the same, I'd hear about it.

He'd hardly gotten settled in his office before he buzzed me in. "Aubrey!"

I rolled my shoulders back and reminded myself that I was a responsible adult. I could hold down a job, even if it was a crappy one. I would work hard and get a promotion and get through this.

I stepped into his crowded, musty office. He had cardboard cut outs and neon clocks and all sorts of promotional paraphernalia displayed from the liquor companies we worked with. All of those extra things added to my claustrophobia, a feeling I would've had even in a larger office, since Isaac was such a creep.

"Hey, Aubrey Longfellow," he said with a leer, "Wanna see my long fellow?"

Exhibit K in my sexual harassment case, should I ever find the courage to file one. I stifled the urge to roll my eyes and instead forced my mouth into a small, toothless smile. "No thank you. Did you need anything?"

He chuckled.

Wrong question. When would I ever learn?

He gave me a specific list of things he "needed," and it took every ounce of will power not to flinch. I kept my smile in place. "Do you need anything work-related?"

"You are no fun, Cupcake," he said with a sigh. "But I do need you to call several beer distributors about the December shipments. Then I need you to download the pictures from the camera and craft them into a calendar we can use as a promotional Christmas gift. Think you can do that?"

"That I can," I said. I was actually pretty good at editing images, if I did say so myself. I'd be sure to photoshop any part of my pictures that got too immodest, not that I intended to let Isaac know that.

He looked up from his phone. "Why are you still standing there?"

"Well, I was wondering if you'd heard anything about the promotion."

He grimaced. "Not yet. It's out of my hands and up to Michaels."

Michaels was his boss and barely an improvement over Isaac. Luckily though, the promotion would at least move me to another warehouse. The commute would be longer, but it would be worth it to get away from Isaac.

"Better get to work on that calendar. Prove to me you're not just a pretty face."

Even though I should've known that he would say something like that, his tone still caught me off guard. It took me a second to gather myself enough to leave his office and get to work on the calendar.

That's when things started to really go downhill.

2

Cole

---

*I*t had been hours since I'd left the mall, but I couldn't quit thinking about Aubrey Longfellow's underwear. I knew they had candy canes on them because I'd seen them in the wash and could recognize the pattern, even from afar. Aubrey was the kind of person who never remembered to get her clothes out of the dryer. She was also the kind of person who would make sure her underwear matched her outfit.

And what an outfit it was. A red velvet dress, ridiculously short with white fur cuffs and white fur on end of the dress. She was wearing these black boots with a high heel, too. Think Mrs. Claus, but make her sexy.

You will not think impure thoughts about your best friend's little sister.

Too late.

But, in my defense, Aubrey was gorgeous, and I'd been without a girlfriend for six months now. This meant I had been without sex for six months because work had kept me entirely too busy. Deidre hadn't been the most effusive of partners, but she had been reliable. That's why I'd proposed to her over the summer.

I had a whole plan. First, I moved into Zach's grandmother's house with plans to buy it eventually. Then, I would propose.

Then we'd have an intimate Christmas wedding. By that time, Aubrey would've grown tired of being the third wheel, and I'd be able to talk her and her brother into selling to me. It was a magical house, an older bungalow with all of the modern renovations, and it was just a short walk from the Marietta Square in a good school district. It would be the perfect place for Deidre and me to raise our two kids—one boy and one girl—and then grow old together.

Just one hitch: Deidre had been shocked by my proposal. She'd thought our relationship wasn't going anywhere. When I confessed that I'd even put out some feelers for a Christmas wedding, she broke the whole thing off with a dismissive, "Apparently, we want different things, Cole."

But that was no reason to be thinking about Aubrey's candy cane underwear. She's my best friend's little sister. There are rules about these things, and I, Cole Frost, am nothing if not a stickler for the rules.

"Yo, Frost, how's the Angelo contract coming?" asked Delray Meeks, my boss.

I frowned. How much time had I been wasting thinking about this morning's incident? "Not good. I still can't figure out what problem he has with the contract."

"Well, you'd better figure it out. Someone leaked our plans to the press, and all of the sports shows are talking about it like it's a done deal."

I groaned. The contract in question was for a reunion of the Atlanta Firebirds 2010 Championship basketball team. Well, the plan was to get the starting five players together at least. We had four signed to an appearance contract, but the fifth, Ezekiel Angelo, was a hold out. That would have been fine if no one knew what we were up to, but someone had blabbed.

In other words, someone hadn't followed the rules.

And this was a big deal, a really big deal. The reunion was part of an ad campaign for a national pizza chain, complete with soft drink company tie-in. There was a huge contest component, and the grand prize was to meet the Firebirds—all of starters, at least—from the 2010 championship team.

"You kidding me, Delray? How'd that happen?"

My boss, a lean six footer who'd played some basketball himself, grimaced. Maybe he could *pretend* to be Ezekiel Angelo. Nah, they didn't look alike at all other than the basics: tall, shaved head, wiry frame, prone to trash talking during any pick up game…

"I don't know, but if I find out who leaked it, their ass is grass. In the meantime, you find whatever it is that has Angelo shook. And fix it."

I ran a hand through my hair—still thick, shouldn't that have counted for something with Deidre?—and picked up the contract once more. Angelo was known for being eccentric. Kinda like if Jeff Goldblum and Charles Barkley had a love child with Lady Gaga tendencies.

Candy Cane Underwear. Just a hint of a round bottom.

I stood calmly and walked past several cubicles to the stairwell. Then I climbed the stairs until I reached the flat roof of our office building. A quick check verified that no one was there.

Then I yelled in frustration, causing a few pigeons to scatter.

I liked to think of it as like Walt Whitman's barbaric yawp that I could sound over the roofs of the world. I'd picked up this habit from my father, an English professor who specialized in midnineteenth century American poetry. Talk over the supper table was always fun in the Frost household.

And by fun, I meant not even the least bit interesting for a child. I don't think my father or stepmother meant to be cold toward me, but neither knew how to relate to a kid. They often got so caught up in their own work that they forgot I was there. Unless, of course, I did something that created a mess. Then I got lectured about logical consequences while I cleaned up my own mess.

Sometimes people asked how I could remain so calm. Pretty sure it had everything to do with screaming on the rooftop where no one could hear me because we were close enough to the traffic on the Loop and the noise of cars. Even better, a train approached on the tracks beside the building.

I yawped one last time as the train hurtled past, its horn melding with my voice.

That accomplished, I went back down the stairs, walked down the hallway at a reasonable pace, and sat back down to study Ezekiel Angelo's contract.

———

About eight hours later, my stomach rumbled to a degree I could no longer ignore.

My phone dinged. It was a text from Delray that simply said, *Frost. Go home.*

Taking a break might help. I gathered my laptop and all of my papers in the satchel that Deidre had gotten me the Christmas before.

Then I sat back down.

What good would it do for me to go home? Aubrey would be there, listening to music that she'd somehow managed to turn up to an eleven. Or she would be banging around while working on an art project in the basement. Or, even worse, trying to teach herself violin.

At this point, it was past time we set some ground rules. But I was paying rent into an account that she and her brother jointly owned, so the least she could do would be to find something quiet to do until I managed to get this contract conundrum sorted out.

I'd bribe her if I had to.

But I needn't have worried. When I got home, she was sitting on the couch watching a movie—at a normal volume. I thought about asking her who she was and what the aliens had done with Aubrey, but she also didn't look over and say hello so I knew she was still mad about the mall incident.

I would've thought flipping me off would've been enough, but apparently not.

And maybe I had overreacted a little bit, but I just…

You didn't want anyone else to see her Candy Cane underwear. Admit it.

True. Neither Zach nor I had been able to protect her from her most recent loser boyfriend, but I sure didn't want pictures of her panties going out into the world.

My eyes caught the box of Kleenex on the coffee table, the pile of wadded up tissues beside it. Surely, she wasn't *that* upset with me. I'd guessed she would've been angry more than sad. I didn't have time to make up with Aubrey, but I found myself putting my satchel in a seat by the table and walking over to where she was watching *The Mummy.*

No wonder the volume was low. She could've recited the entire movie if she'd wanted to. Heck, I could recite most of *The Mummy* by now. It was the movie she played when she was sad, when she was mad, when she was happy, and when she was bored. She would watch it in the rain or on a train or in a boat or with a goat.

But the tissues said sad and I got a pang in my chest, an invisible knife of pain. "Aubrey, are you okay?"

She shook her head no.

"Wanna talk about it?"

She shook her head no.

"Want me to just sit here and watch Brendan Fraser fight mummies with you?"

She shook her head yes.

There were about a thousand things I needed to do rather than watch this movie for the millionth time. Conversation would've been more productive.

Finally, as the music swelled and the credits started, she reached for the remote and turned off the television.

"Now you want to talk about it?"

She looked at me, her eyes finally dry but still red, as was the tip of her nose. I wanted to punch whoever had made her cry, and it was going to be awkward if that someone was me.

After a shuddering breath, she spoke, "This has been an awful day. I don't want to talk about it."

Whenever Aubrey said *I don't want to talk about it,* it meant she definitely wanted to talk about it. I waited.

"First, you got on my case. Then my boss was…himself. Then the photos for the calendar were ruined, and my boss yelled at me for a solid ten minutes—I timed it. Then I got a flat tire on the way home, and some asshole splashed me with muddy water while I was waiting for Triple A. When I got home, I saw I'd forgotten to pay one of my bills, and now I have a late fee. I tripped while reading said bill and scraped my knee on the sidewalk. To top it all off, Kevin was here so I had to tell him off while blood ran down my leg, and you know how I feel about blood. I wasn't about to let him into the house."

My heart rate increased at the mention of Kevin. He was the aforementioned loser ex. "But he's gone?"

"And I told him not to come back."

She'd also bandaged her knee, so that was taken care of.

"I'm sorry I added to your crappy day," I said softly.

Her lips turned up slightly, threatening a smile. "You did get the ball rolling."

"Yeah, it's none of my business if you want to show off your candy cane underwear."

Her eyes widened. "You could see the candy canes?"

I nodded.

She exhaled sharply. "I didn't even want to have my picture taken like that, but I'm trying to prove that I can hold down a job. I'm so tired of being the loser slacker of the family."

"You're not the loser slacker of the family," I said.

"Oh come on, Cole. You know you've thought it, too. What's Aubrey done now? Why can't she finish her degree? Why does she keep getting fired from jobs? Why is she going out with yet another loser? At least I provide plenty of gossip for the otherwise perfect Longfellow family."

I swallowed hard. I had said some of those things, but to hear her say them now, I was pretty damn ashamed of myself. "Aubrey, you just…think outside the box."

She arched an eyebrow and tilted her head to one side, indicting me with her eyes.

"And you've had some bad luck."

"Really?"

I stood and began pacing. "Okay, fine. You have made some decisions I wouldn't have made. There. Is that what you wanted to hear?"

"Yes, actually. But it was very sweet of you to reassure me first. Thank you."

Her gratitude stopped me in my tracks. It might have been the most civil conversation we'd had in months. Probably the most civil conversation since back in high school when we both teamed up against Zach because he had the unfortunate opinion that *Mamma Mia!* wasn't a good movie. Aubrey and I had sung "Waterloo" over and over again until he cried uncle.

I had no regrets.

"I think I'm going to bed. Maybe tomorrow will be better."

I watched her trail down the hall. The house was about to be quiet so I could think, but unease still churned in my gut. Was that worry I was feeling? For Aubrey?

Cole, you need to worry about yourself.

So true and yet…

I carried my satchel to the little table in the kitchen and made a pot of coffee. I had a lot of fine-print reading to do.

3

Aubrey

I called in sick the next day.

Was this the responsible thing to do?

No, absolutely not.

Did I need a mental health day?

Oh, yes. I most certainly did.

Sure, Cole had been surprising comforting the night before, but I still needed to get myself together.

I'd been thinking about the Not So Naughty List and Mercury in retrograde and the spectacularly craptastic day I'd had yesterday. Rationally, I knew the two couldn't be related, but, then again, I'd rarely been accused of being rational. If I had a dollar for every time the words "free spirit" had been used to describe me, then I wouldn't have to go back to my ridiculously crappy job.

And on that subject, something weird happened at the office yesterday. The pictures of me sitting on Santa's lap had been ruined. All of the other pictures had downloaded just fine, but not a one of the pictures of me and Santa had been clear. Isaac *claimed* that they'd been just fine when he checked them. He was convinced that I'd done something to them. Then he yelled at me for ruining his calendar—for ten minutes straight.

A little nagging part of me remembered how Santa didn't like the provocative outfit or the bottle of tequila on my hip, and I hadn't been that comfortable with it, either. So if he were the real Santa, he'd probably have some kind of way to mess with the image…

If he were the real Santa. Do you even hear yourself, Aubrey?

The doorbell rang.

I opened the door to Mrs. Potts, our neighbor to the left. She's an older woman who'd dyes her hair purple and likes to wear her eyeglasses on a rhinestone chain, so naturally she was one of my favorite folks in the neighborhood.

"Mrs. Potts, come on in!"

"No time, dear. But the mailman put this in my box by mistake." She handed me an envelope before starting to back away slowly. "Don't shoot the messenger!"

She was already speed walking down the sidewalk as I turned over the envelope to see…a jury duty summons?

That was it. There had to be a way to get off this so-called Not-So-Naughty List, and I was going to find it.

ONCE I GOT TO THE MALL, SANTA WAS OFF "FEEDING HIS REINDEER."

Of course he was.

After a few minutes, he returned along with the older woman in the green elf costume. I leaned over the fence. "Excuse me, could I speak with Santa for a minute?"

She gestured to a line full of mothers and preschoolers, many of whom were starting to fuss. "You'll have to wait in line like everybody else."

I took a deep breath and got in line. At least I could make faces at the cute baby in front of me. When the baby fell asleep, I counted the number of mothers and children ahead of me. I could only guess, but there appeared to be twenty family units in line before I would get to Santa. People were beginning to line up behind me, too.

I kinda needed to pee, but I also wanted coffee.

Who'd have thought that all of these people would be here? Don't these moms have to work? Why aren't there more stay-at-home dads? I need to remember to make this trip in November when I have kids.

When I had kids.

Something suspiciously like my biological clock began ticking somewhere in my belly.

No, no, no, no.

I was not about to go looking for a new relationship just because I wanted kids. I was twenty-eight. I still had time. I had promised myself that I would work on me and not worry about being in a relationship.

I looked up at the big, red velvet throne. Santa had arrived, and the line began to slowly move.

My damned biological clock pulsed inside my belly as I watched kids sit in Santa's lap and look up at him in wonder. Even the ones who screamed their fool heads off seemed cute to me.

Aubrey, I swear you are the hottest of messes.

Yeah, well, I was a hot mess with a tire that still needed to be changed and a summons to jury duty. That was more than enough adulting for anyone.

Although…jury duty would get me away from Isaac. That was something to consider.

We inched our way through unrolled cotton that was supposed to be snow and past candy canes that served as queue markers. With five more family units to go, those pesky reindeer needed to be fed again so Santa ambled off for a well-deserved break.

"Could you please hold my spot in line?" the mother in front of me asked. "I really need to change her diaper."

The cutie I'd earlier been making faces with had woken up with a scowl. I had no choice but to say, "Absolutely."

The mother left her stroller in front of me but then took anything of value. I wanted to be offended at the implication that I might steal anything of hers, but what did I know about babies? Maybe she needed all of those accoutrements.

I shifted from foot to foot. Good thing I'd taken the day off because this errand was taking forever. In front of me, a husband appeared with a Starbucks cup. He opened his arms for their baby; his wife took the coffee.

I felt such a pulse of longing.

Cole would be the kind of husband to bring you coffee and then hold the baby.

My face flushed there in the line to see Santa. Where in heaven's name had that thought come from? Cole and I could hardly share a house without getting irritated with each other. He was so not my type.

Yes, because your type has worked out so well in the past.

The mother in front of me returned and thanked me profusely as she settled the baby in the stroller and stored her diaper bag and purse and such.

"Hey!" said the woman behind me. "No cutting!"

I turned around. "She didn't cut in line. She's been here the whole time. She just had to change the baby's diaper."

"You're lying."

"No," I said. "I promise. I watched the stroller for her."

The harried woman behind me had a child swinging on each arm. Her face grew progressively redder. "Well, we should get to go first because we didn't leave the line."

"That's ridiculous," I sputtered while the mother in front of me said, "Go ahead. I've only got one child."

That, of course, meant one more family between me and Santa, but I bit my tongue. I might be having a run of bad luck, but I was going to take it with some grace, dammit.

Santa returned, but something about him seemed…off.

Sure enough, when I finally got up there, he wasn't the same Santa. His beard was too blonde. I looked from him to the elf photographer and back. She sourly asked, "Are you getting your picture taken or not?"

"Yeah! Hurry up. Some of us have kids," someone said from the line that had wound its way back to the pretzel place.

"Ho ho ho, what do you want for Christmas, little girl?"

I sat down tentatively and smiled for the picture before saying, "I want to be taken off the Not So Nice list."

"Ho ho, I'm sure a pretty girl such as yourself isn't naughty."

"I'm not. I'm on the Not So Nice List."

He handed me a tiny candy cane and then whispered, "Just move along. I have a lot of *children* to see."

Dazed and most definitely confused, I stepped over to the counter. The older elf had moved over to talk about photo packages and had turned the camera over to a woman with dreadlocks and a blinding smile.

"You're back, huh?" the elf said.

Hope bloomed in spite of her sour expression.

"Yes. Do you know where the other Santa is?"

"The North Pole. Are you interested in a photo package?"

"No, I need to know how to get off this so called Not So Naughty List," I said, not caring if she thought I was crazy. People thought I was crazy all the time. I would do whatever it took to stop my recent run of bad luck.

She put down a sheet of sample photos as if discussing packages with me. "Maybe I can tell you if you buy a photo package."

"Is this some kind of elf extortion?"

She drew back the samples and started to walk away.

"No, no, no. I'll buy a package. I don't know what's going on, but I have to figure out how to undo it."

"Well, it's simple, actually. You're going to have to do three selfless things for that young man you flipped off."

"Why three?"

"Because I believe you wished three bad things on him. Also, three, as you should've learned from *Schoolhouse Rock*, is a magic number."

I groaned.

She gave me a death stare. "Will it be the deluxe package then?"

"No, please. Uh, how about that middle one?" I pointed at a

more reasonable one. She clicked a few buttons and rang me up. When she returned with the photos fresh from the printer, she handed me a sleigh bell on a red velvet cord.

"Put this on your wall or some place where it won't ring by accident. If you can make it ring three times before Christmas Day, then you'll find yourself back on the Nice List."

"I took my photos in one hand and the bell in the other. "But what if I can't?"

She shook her head sadly. "Then you're in for a whole year of bad luck."

Once home again, I surveyed the scene. Something selfless for Cole…

Ugh. Why should I have to do something selfless for him just because I flipped him off—he shouldn't have been looking at my underwear. And he *should* get that stick out of his ass, and he *should* mind his own business, and he *should* get out of my house.

Okay, so technically my underwear was out there for him and everybody else to see, so he wasn't exactly prying into my business. Now that I thought about it, his expression hadn't telegraphed disapproval so much as concern. And I'd flipped him off because I was embarrassed. Just the thought of Cole seeing my underwear made me blush.

Nope. No. Not going there. I needed to work on me. I'd identified two things key to being a responsible adult. One, I had to hold down a job even if it was boring or soul sucking. Two, I had to learn how to live without a boyfriend. The six months since I finally left Kevin had been the longest I'd gone in years without one, but I'd had a string of losers, guys who liked the idea of me but not the real me. That had to stop.

As for getting Cole out of the house? It wasn't *my* house. Grandma had left it to both Zach and me. Then Zach had moved off to North Carolina. I'd needed place to live, but he'd already been renting the place to Cole. Cozy, huh?

I surveyed the house. I'd left a pair of shoes in the corner. The kitchen table chairs each had one of my sweatshirts hanging from them. I hadn't done the dishes from the night before. There were stacks of papers and craft projects around the living room as well as several books I'd started but not finished.

Okay, so maybe Cole was right about one thing. It would appear I had some slightly slobbish tendencies. And I hadn't even considered all of the toiletries I had strewn across the vanity in the bathroom or the laundry I hadn't taken out of the dryer. Or all of the other craft projects in the basement.

But cleaning up wasn't really *selfless*. I mean, as much as I hated to clean, I enjoyed a clean house and the smell of Fabuloso as much as the next girl.

I slumped down into one of the kitchen chairs. What then? I couldn't get the man a puppy. The spoilsport wouldn't even let me get a kitten. You didn't even have to take a kitten outside for walks or bathroom time.

Such a killjoy.

Aubrey, stop it. You have to think nice thoughts about Cole, so you can think of something selfless to do for him. Otherwise, who knows what comes after jury duty?

I took a few deep, cleansing breaths.

I closed my eyes and searched my memory banks for times when Cole and Zach had played together as boys or hung out at teens. What would Cole Frost *like*?

My eyes popped open.

Of course!

He spent almost all of December with our family because his father and stepmother were usually too busy arguing with each other to celebrate Christmas. He especially liked to come here after school. He would sit in the light of the Christmas tree until his stepmother called him home for supper or our bedtime, whichever came first.

Even as a girl, I had wondered how parents could not notice that one of their children hadn't come home from school. But Grandma would help him with his homework, just as she did with Zach and me. She gave him the same milk and cookies.

No wonder Cole wants to buy this house from you.

He could talk about location and school districts and the proximity to work all he liked, but there was a part of him deep down that wanted to live here because it was a place where he'd been happy.

To be honest, there was no need to kick him out. Neither one of us had a significant other we wanted to marry. We had plenty of room to share. When I thought about it from the point of view that the house was just as much, if not more, a home to him, then it made it easier not to be as annoyed with him.

I smiled to myself, knowing exactly what my first selfless act for Cole was going to be.

A clean house and Christmas decorations, coming up!

4

Cole

It was after seven when I finally made it home. I paused outside the front door. Was that Christmas music? Yes! Aubrey was playing the old Mariah Carey Christmas album. Per usual, it was loud enough for the entire neighborhood to enjoy.

I took a deep breath and steeled myself for whatever elaborate craft mess she had begun. But when I opened the door, the house was…clean.

I stopped in the foyer looking over to the kitchen. Clean—except for the tray of cookies fresh from the oven. And the table was cleared of clutter and had been wiped down to a shine. Beyond me, the living room was free of shoes and books and stacks of paper. I sucked in a breath.

She'd put up the Christmas tree, and multicolored lights reflected on the ceiling. It reminded me of being younger, back when this was Miss Ruth's house.

"Hey, Mister Tall Man," Aubrey yelled over the music. "Would you mind putting the angel on top?"

I swallowed hard.

She stepped down from the chair, and I stepped up. She handed me the angel, and I placed her on top of the tree. It was one of those seemingly mundane moments in life that you wanted to freeze and capture forever because you felt as though you were exactly where you were supposed to be doing exactly what you were supposed to be doing.

Miss Ruth used to let me put the angel on the tree. She knew my dad and stepmom were too busy fighting to decorate a tree. She'd always wait until one of those evenings when my stepmonster didn't even call to check on me—she never had to wait long—and then she'd say, "Young Master Cole, do you think you could stand on that chair and put the angel on the tree for me?"

For years I thought it was because she was afraid to stand on the chair. Only later did I realize that she wanted me to have something important to do, something that was all my own. It was a kindness I've never forgotten even if I'd somehow fallen into my parents' trap of not decorating for Christmas.

"You've been busy," I said as I stepped down from the chair and followed Aubrey into the kitchen. I didn't know what else to say.

"Cookie?"

"Sure."

Oh. It was one of those peanut butter cookies with the chocolate kiss on top, my favorite. A groan of pleasure escaped me.

"Your favorite, right?"

My eyes narrowed. She wanted something. There was no other explanation for the cleaning, the decorating, and the cookies. "What do you want?"

Her eyes filled with hurt, and I could've kicked myself.

"Nothing. I just thought..."

I waited for her to finish her sentence while Mariah sang about what wonderful a child Jesus was. The bounce of the song didn't match the slump in Aubrey's shoulders.

"Hey, I didn't mean that," I said. "I appreciate the cookie. And the decorating. And all of the cleaning, too."

A ghost of a smile returned, and she shrugged. "I had the day off so I thought it was high time we got into the spirit. Wanna watch a Christmas movie with some hot chocolate?"

Yeah, I kinda did.

But I couldn't.

"I would like to, but I have to work. I still haven't figured out what's wrong with this contract."

"Oh."

Was she actually disappointed that I didn't want to sit down and watch a movie with her? Usually we barely acknowledged each other's presence when one of us arrived home.

"I'll, uh, put these cookies away and go work in the basement then," she said as she walked over to Miss Ruth's ancient stereo system and cut off the music.

Out of nowhere a bell rang, and she grinned. The way the smile lit up her face took my breath away. Before I could fully process that feeling, she had gone downstairs. I took another cookie and sat down at the table to look over the cursed contract yet again.

I'D BEEN WORKING FOR AN HOUR, AND IT WAS SO QUIET I COULD almost hear a lack of sound. It was odd, very odd. Usually, Aubrey had to have the television on. Or the stereo. Or she'd be singing along with her headphones. Or sawing away at her violin.

I ran a hand through my hair in frustration.

Of course!

Ezekiel Angelo was well known for having odd riders added to his appearance contracts, and it was common knowledge that he'd added a new one as of late: Beethoven. Why Beethoven? I did not know, but I remember a friend of mine who worked for our soft drink company partner telling me about how they had to have Beethoven playing in the green room.

I pumped a fist and hastily sent an email to Ezekiel's agent, saying that I would be happy to add a rider about Beethoven to the contract. Not a one of the other former players had a stipulation about *not* playing music, so it shouldn't be a problem.

My elation was short-lived.

No, it was more that it had been replaced with a different feeling. I itched to share my news with someone.

I should probably check on Aubrey anyway, to make sure something hadn't happened to her. After all, I didn't know she was capable of being quiet for this long.

But first…

I puttered around the kitchen gathering the ingredients for hot chocolate and then knocked on the basement door. "Aubrey? Still up for that movie?"

She didn't answer. That wasn't like her at all. I knocked again, louder this time.

Now I was getting concerned.

I took a deep breath and went down the stairs. She stood at an easel with her back to the door. Music spilled from her headphones, and she bobbed her head in time with the beat while she worked.

She was painting a sleigh bell like the one I'd heard earlier, only she'd really captured the shadow and light. She'd placed the bell slightly off center. It was a ridiculously engaging painting for the simplicity of the subject.

Along the wall were stacked several canvases where she'd been trying modern styles and landscapes, portraits and surrealism. On a table to the back were stacks of paintings she'd made on glass. She'd experimented with wood and ceramics too.

It felt as though I were looking into Aubrey's mind, and it was a place that dazzled with a million ideas she hadn't yet figured out how to implement.

When she paused in her painting, I lightly touched her shoulder, and she startled so hard she almost dropped her brush.

"Good Lord, you scared me half to death," she said, clutching her chest. Well, she yelled it because she was still wearing the headphones. After a couple of deep breaths, she removed them and then pushed a button on her phone that stopped the music.

Naturally, she'd slung little bits of paint everywhere in the process.

"Sorry. I got concerned when you didn't answer my knock," I said.

She gave me a sheepish grin. "You mean to say you were concerned about little ol' me?"

"Yes. I, ah, think I figured out what was wrong with the contract. I can make hot chocolate now."

"Tell me more," she said in a low voice that made my breath catch.

"Well, I wondered if you were still up for that Christmas movie."

"Only if I get to pick."

I shrugged. "Sure."

I left her to clean up her workspace—something she actually did this time—and went upstairs to make the cocoa. Soon we settled into the living room with our mugs and cookies to watch a movie. We'd never really done that before. Usually, she watched her programs or I watched mine. Occasionally, we'd be in the same room for Braves games, but she preferred to sit on the floor and craft on those nights.

Suddenly, Miss Ruth's love seat felt a little smaller. *Love seat*, the words rang out in my head. We were sitting on a love seat. I'd been harboring some pretty adult thoughts about Aubrey's candy cane underwear and now we were sitting together on a *love* seat, which made me think about making love, which made me wonder what kinds of sounds Aubrey might make if I kissed that spot just above her collarbone and…

Stop it. She's your best friend's little sister.

Besides, it would never work out. Today's whirlwind cleaning aside, the woman drove me crazy with how she left her shoes wherever she kicked them off or how she didn't see the need to do dishes immediately after a meal. Heck, I was lucky she hadn't flung paint on me earlier.

Suddenly Hugh Grant was talking about airports, and I held in a groan. I remembered this movie well because I'd watched it again with Deidre last Christmas. The last thing I needed to do was to sit on a love seat with Aubrey Longfellow while watching a movie that included, among other sexy premises, porn extras. Did she do this on purpose?

"Oh, wait," she said, her face an adorable shade of pink. "This movie is kinda long. Maybe The Grinch?"

I cleared my throat. The Grinch would be much better. "Uh, yeah. But the animated one."

"Of course," she said with a tone of voice that suggested there were no other versions of *How the Grinch Stole Christmas*, and I heartily agreed with her on that assessment.

"Thanks for the hot chocolate," she said at about the time The Grinch started formulating his plan.

"Sure. It was your idea," I said, taking a larger gulp than I meant to. I put my cup on the coffee table and leaned back on the couch. I sat to the left; she sat to the right. My right hand was mere inches from her left hand. My fingers twitched.

She stared at the television—like I should be doing—but I couldn't help but study her profile. Her nose had a slight bump on the bridge from where she broke it playing basketball with Zach and me. She hated that bump, but I thought it gave her character. She also hated her freckles, but I loved those, too. Her lips begged to be kissed…

Cole! Eyes on the television.

And the Grinch's heart wasn't the only thing in danger of growing three sizes, so I glued my eyes back to the screen.

But here's the thing about The Grinch: it's not long. Soon, we were sitting in the living room with nothing to do. Was it just my imagination or did she not want to leave the living room anymore than I did?

"Well," she said. "That certainly got me into the Christmas spirit."

"Makes you want to go down and rob an entire village of their decorations and presents and roast beast, huh?"

She laughed, as I'd hoped she would.

"Seriously, though," I said. "Thanks for all of your decorating and the cookies and everything."

Her smile widened and she shrugged. "Just thought it might be a nice thing to do."

"It was," I said.

"Is there anything else you really like to do for Christmas?" she asked with some hesitation. "I hadn't moved in yet last year, and I don't want to cramp your style this year."

The only thing I'd recently done for Christmas was split a bottle of white wine with Deidre while we watched *Love Actually* followed by…sex.

But I couldn't tell Aubrey that. I cleared my throat to make sure the suggestion stayed in my mind where it belonged. "I should be asking you the same question."

She shrugged again. "Nothing really. I have a few more snacks to make, but I'm pretty set."

Was that disappointment I felt knotting up behind my breastbone? No way was I going to start buying gifts for Aubrey. Heck, the only thing I knew she wanted was a kitten, which, no way. Deidre was allergic to cats. Okay, so I wasn't seeing Deidre anymore, but the next woman I dated might be allergic to cats too. Besides, I'd never had a pet before. I didn't know what to do with one. Not that I was about to admit that to Aubrey.

"Well, I guess I'll go to bed since I have to get up early for work."

"Sure," she said.

Just as I was about to head down the hall, I stopped. "You know. My real mom used to make something called Nuts and Bolts. It's kinda like Chex Mix. Sometimes I miss it."

She smiled. "Interesting."

"Good night," I said, not knowing what to add and feeling ridiculously awkward about the whole thing.

5

Aubrey

*N*uts and Bolts.

I'd googled it and found several recipes, but which one was the closest to what Cole was talking about? And would my efforts at tracking down the right recipe make my sleigh bell jingle?

That sounded kinda dirty.

To be honest, for half a second last night, I'd wanted Cole to jingle my bells. His eyes had twinkled behind his glasses, and his lips had turned up into a smile. For half a second, I felt that same jolt I'd felt as a teenager whenever he'd been around. It had to be because I almost subjected him to *Love Actually*, a movie that has more than one set of boobs and lots of people having sex or wanting to have sex or pretending to have sex in it. I had to have been losing my mind to have suggested it.

Just because Cole Frost was objectively attractive did not mean that the two of us would make a good match. If I wanted to live under the gaze of someone's constant disapproval, then I could move in with my parents. Perish the thought.

Thank goodness I'd remembered all of the sexy times before we got too far into the movie because that would've been *awkward*.

Even better, I'd gotten the first jingle out of that blasted bell.

Only it wasn't for all of the cleaning or the decorating; it was for saying I'd go to the basement and leave Cole alone. I mean, was I really that loud?

No, but you're Naughty List adjacent, so it only makes sense you would have to go to your room. Or the basement, as it were.

A smarter person wouldn't be playing into any of this, but I'd managed to avoid another flat tire and jury duty today, so I was going to continue with Operation Get Off the Not So Nice List.

The fact that Cole had been so happy with the cookies and the decorations was really its own reward. When I saw the look of wonder in his eyes when he walked through the door, it was almost like a present for me. How could I have forgotten how much time he spent with our family and with Grandma?

"Aubrey," Isaac said from his office door. "How's the calendar coming?"

"I sent you some PDFs for approval," I said.

"What about Miss December?"

I smiled. "I had to improvise a little, but I think it'll work."

He grunted and adjusted himself.

That promotion had to come at the end of this journey because, vow or no vow, I was not going to be able to work for that man much longer.

As for the Miss December picture? I'd set my phone on a tripod and set a timer to take pictures of me in the skimpy dress with the bottle of tequila in front of the tree before Cole got home. Santa wasn't included. No one could see my underwear—thank goodness—but I was pretty sure I'd captured the essence of what Isaac wanted.

Two turtledoves with one stone, that's what I called that.

Except for the part where the turtledoves might get hurt, because I wasn't on board with animal cruelty.

"Good work," he shouted from his office. "Send it to the printer and see if you can sweet talk them into getting it by next week without making it a rush job."

I exhaled. Sure. Right. Because the print shop he wanted me to use was run by a guy very similar to him. Fortunately, Allen had a fondness for low-cut shirts and high-end liquor. Even more fortunately, we happened to have some high-end liquor lying around for occasions such as this. I also happened to be wearing a low-cut shirt because, hey, you gotta highlight your assets.

Unfortunately, the sweet talking and the liquor required a visit to the print shop rather than a simple call or email.

I grabbed my purse and was about to push my chair under the table when a tall blonde woman walked through the door. "Excuse me, is this High Spirits Liquor Distributors?"

"Yes," I said.

"I'm looking for an Isaac Gibson about a possible job?"

I smiled widely. He must be hiring her for my position. With her sleek hair, tight clothes and manicured nails, she would be what most men considered an upgrade on this current secretarial model.

But I didn't care.

Because that meant I was going to be promoted.

"He's right through there," I said, pausing only to use the phone—like a civilized person—to tell Isaac that he had a job applicant. He'd already seen her through the glass of his office wall and was gesturing her in.

For a split second, I wondered if I should stay behind and chaperone. Maybe at least warn the poor woman?

No, he usually behaved during the job interview. If she got the position, I could give her the lowdown before I moved on. I had a printer to persuade.

6

Cole

I found myself humming Christmas carols, especially "You're a Mean One, Mr. Grinch." Things were definitely looking up, and I didn't even mind sharing the house with Aubrey as much as I had before. Sure, my attraction to her was inconvenient, but she'd been so kind about all of the decorations and even about letting me work in peace.

And look what had happened? I'd come up with the solution for the contract and had time left over to watch a movie with her. Maybe she and I could learn to coexist after all.

"What the heck are you humming?" Delray asked as he stepped inside by office. He folded his large frame into the chair on the other side of my desk.

"My roommate wanted to watch The Grinch last night, and now I have an ear worm," I said.

"Your roommate? What is she, twelve?"

I waved him off. I didn't have time for any kind of male posturing about things that were childish. I needed to get to work on all of my end of the year reports because Christmas Eve was our last day in the office. Anything not finalized by then wouldn't count toward the bonus I'd receive early next year. Even though I wasn't planning to marry Deidre now, I was more than earning the bonus that would come my way. Maybe I'd take myself on a tropical vacation.

Or I'd save it as a down payment on a house because I was nothing if not pragmatic.

"Listen, you got the Angelo thing ironed out?"

My phone buzzed. "Oh, look. There's Ezekiel Angelo's agent now."

Delray motioned for me to take the call, and I put it on speakerphone.

"What's up, Luis? Are we a go?"

After a pause, Luis finally said, "We need to talk."

"Uh-oh. It's not me, it's you, isn't it?"

Delray snorted from his perch across from my desk, and I help up a finger to shush him.

"Come on, Cole. You know I'm rooting for you, but he still won't sign the papers."

My fingers paused over my laptop keys. "But I figured out the Beethoven rider."

"Well, he said to tell you good guess, but that's not it. He also said to tell you he's rooting for you to figure it out."

And Delray thought my roommate was being childish. I took a deep breath. "This is so frustrating. Why won't he just tell me what he wants, so I can make it happen? You know I will."

Luis sighed. "Look, Ezekiel Angelo is so great to work for, but, like a lot of people who come into a significant amount of money, he has a hard time knowing whom he can trust. He likes to make sure people respect him enough to go that extra mile to understand him."

"And you're positive it's not a bowl of only green m&ms?"

Luis chuckled. "Positive."

"All right," I said with a sigh. "I'm back at it. I'm going to figure this out or die trying."

"That's the spirit!" Luis said.

We said our goodbyes and ended the call. Delray stared

through me with a look that suggested I'd better figure out what silly thing Ezekiel Angelo wanted.

I could feel the need to yawp coming on. Bad day for it, too, because the temperature had dropped overnight, and the sky was spitting something euphemistically called a wintry mix.

I closed my laptop with more force than was strictly necessary. "Why won't he just tell me, Delray?"

"I don't know, but you can ask him at the company party tonight."

I groaned.

"You forgot, didn't you?"

Forgot? More like intentionally filed it away in the dark recesses of my mind. I didn't want to see Deidre at the Christmas Party with her new man, the one she'd gotten engaged to about five minutes after meeting him. I was over her, I swear I was, but that didn't take the sting out of being replaced so easily.

"Frost, your ass needs to be there, and you'd better bring a date. Last week, Angelo told ESPN in an interview that he doesn't trust bachelors."

"That's ridiculous!"

Delray shrugged. "Of course, it's ridiculous. I swear he says all this stuff just to see who's really paying attention to him."

"Fine. I will be there."

"With a date."

"Yeah, yeah. With a date." If a blow-up doll counted as a date. Or Mrs. Potts. She might be free. No, Angelo probably didn't trust men with Oedipal complexes, and, really, who could blame him on that one?

Delray got up with a little grunt, which told me the wintry mix was jacking with his bum knee. "I'm counting on you, Frost. I gave you this account because I thought you were the best person to handle it. Don't prove me wrong."

"I won't." My browser was already filled with every article and interview I could find on Ezekiel Angelo. If he wanted someone who listened to him, then I would be that guy.

But first I had to find a date.

I smacked my forehead. Of course! Aubrey would be a great date.

If she were willing and if she were free.

But would she take it the wrong way? Would she think I was asking her on an actual date? Did I want to ask her on a date?

No, you do not. She's your best friend's little sister, which is a bullshit patriarchal concept, but one that you will adhere to for the time being. You promised Zach that you would look after her.

Which was also a bullshit patriarchal concept, but I really didn't have time to fight the patriarchy today, since I needed to figure out what was wrong with this contract. And to get a date, which led me right back to the pernicious patriarchy.

Tomorrow I would rededicate myself to fighting the patriarchy. For now? Well, I needed to call Aubrey and see if I could talk her into being my date to the Christmas party.

7

Aubrey

It took forever to get back from the print shop where Allen had been a gentleman on the whole. For the most part, he was just pleased with his single barrel bourbon gift set. He'd also been happy to print the calendar for us without a rush fee, and he hadn't even ogled my cleavage too much.

That was the good news.

The bad news was that I'd gotten another flat tire, which meant a trip to a garage. Even worse? My two remaining tires were bald, so I had to get a set of four. Then Isaac had bitched me out for not coming straight back. He didn't care if I ruined my rims.

The Not So Nice List had struck again.

There was no sign of the woman I'd left behind, and I wasn't about to start asking questions. Best to keep my head down and work on double-checking our shipment information. We'd be having a busy next few weeks since Christmas led straight into New Year's. Dryuary would give me a little break, even though it usually put Isaac in a foul mood. He wanted people to keep drinking all year long.

No one's liver could handle that.

My cell phone started playing "Shake it Off," which was the song I'd assigned to Cole, mainly to remind me to shake it off when he lectured me about leaving the milk on the counter or forgetting to pay the water bill or whatever.

Usually, I'd ignore him at least once, but I caught myself smiling. "Mr. Frost."

"Ms. Longfellow."

He had a nice phone voice, as smooth as the bourbon I'd given away earlier. How had I not noticed that before? And his pause was cute. He was going to ask me for something. He always paused before asking for a favor because he hated to ask for favors.

"I, uh…"

"Spit it out, Cole. What can I do you for?"

I winced. No need to take my foul mood out on him.

"Well, uh, my company is having a Christmas party, and I was wondering if you could come as my plus one."

He started carrying on about Ezekiel Angelo and something about how the man didn't trust bachelors, but I zoned out a little because, of all the things I thought he might ask me, being his plus one for a swanky Christmas party had never crossed my mind.

"I mean, I know it's short notice. Really short notice. I mean, I'm sure you have plans. I'm sorry I bothered you. I'll just—"

"Wait a minute. Ezekiel Angelo is going to be there?"

He was my favorite basketball player ever.

"Yes, and—"

"I'll go," I said quickly before he could hang up. A party? Free food? A chance to see Ezekiel Angelo? Why not?

"Really?"

"Yes, really. What's the dress code?"

"Uh, something nice?"

Lord, give me strength.

I had yet to meet a man who understood the intricacies of a woman's wardrobe. "Formal? Semi-Formal? Cocktail? Casual?"

I could almost envision him pushing up his glasses just enough to pinch the bridge of his nose in exasperation even if such a thing was impossible. "I think I remember seeing something about Semi-Formal?"

"I've got that. I can meet you there or are you picking me up at the house?"

"Uh, could you possibly get a Lyft to the Hotel Madison and be there at six-thirty? Then, obviously, I'll drive you home."

The Madison? The fancy hotel out by the new baseball stadium? Okay. "I can do that."

He sighed with relief. "You are a lifesaver, Aubrey. I really owe you one."

A lifesaver? Surely that had to count for something with that old sleigh bell.

What if it rings and you aren't there to hear it?

I murmured my goodbyes as I pondered the question. Was it like the old tree falling in the forest thing? But seriously, what if that was one of my selfless acts, and I didn't even know it because I didn't have the bell with me?

I'd have to start keeping that bell with me at all times.

Once home, I tried to decide between the black sheath and the red strapless dress with a flowy, fluffy tulle skirt.

Eh, why not go with the red? It had sparkles on the bodice and a cute little faux belt with a rhinestone buckle. Plus, red was a better color for me. And I also had a velvet shrug to keep me warm on the way. Well, warm adjacent, but I was just going from house to car to hotel.

But what if you embarrass Cole?

Embarrass him? What about this little red dress would embarrass him? My mind replayed things my mother had said to me, things my ex had said, and even things that my high school algebra teacher had said: "Aubrey, can't you calm down a little? Can't you dress more like an adult? Why do you always have to be the center of attention? Don't you think that dress shows too much skin?"

The voices swirled in my head, and I reached for the staid black sheath dress, a classic LBD that I could've worn to a funeral.

No.

When I finally kicked Kevin to the curb, I promised myself that I would do only what I wanted to do. I would stop thinking about how anyone else wanted me to act or be or dress.

But you're supposed to be doing selfless things, remember?

Well, if Cole wanted me to come to this party, then he wanted me to come as just the person I was. Besides, he'd seemed desperate enough to take me in sweats, so the red dress it would be.

Come to think of it, he'd never really been on my case as much as other people in my life. Not really. Oh, he wanted me to do my share of the dishes and wished my shoes wouldn't clutter the living room, but he would've expected that from anyone.

Never before had I considered such things from his point of view. Of course, I'd spent a good idea of my life preemptively cringing, just waiting for whatever my mom would get on my case for next.

Shaking off any thoughts of my mother, I jumped into the shower and shampooed and shaved and did all of the things. Next, I worked with my unruly hair, deciding on an elegant updo to better show off my shoulders. Makeup? Dramatic. Lotion? With teeny flecks of glitter. Come on, this was a party!

Stepping into the dress, I called for the Lyft and then raced around to get shoes and accessories as a driver headed my way immediately. I found a clutch and grabbed the jingle bell to put inside. I wasn't going to miss it if it rang this time.

<hr>

8

Cole

<hr>

I beat Aubrey to the party and stood by the door waiting nervously. She'd texted me to say she was on the way, but I still wasn't prepared when she walked into the ballroom.

I drew in a breath at her red dress. It had no sleeves—not even straps—and a short puffy-looking skirt. She had her black hair all twisted up and wore more makeup than she usually did. The combination of shorter skirt and higher heels did fantastic things for her legs.

When her eyes locked with mine, she grinned, and it knocked the breath right out of me.

Best friend's little sister—

Oh, shut up. She's a grown woman.

As she walked to me with such purpose, I had the impulse to look over my shoulder. Surely, she couldn't be there for me. And I had invited her!

About a yard away, she twirled. "Do I clean up nicely or what?"

"You are beautiful," I said, my voice cracking on the last word.

"You don't look so bad yourself," she said. "Except for those bags under your eyes. You're working too hard."

"Well, I have more work ahead of me. I can't figure out what is making Ezekiel Angelo unhappy about this contract. It wasn't what I thought," I said as I led her toward the buffet.

"Why don't you let me look at it?" she asked. When I gaped at her, she added, "Unless it's confidential or something."

"No. I mean, yes, but I don't know why you'd want to read the legalese. Unless you have some kind of insomnia problem I don't know about."

"No, silly. I just happen to be one of Ezekiel Angelo's biggest fans."

"Well, you're going to get to meet him tonight."

"Meet him?" she asked as she grabbed a plate. The way her eyes widened and her mouth formed an O of shock was utterly adorable.

"I'm not kidding." I nodded my head to the right. "He's right over there."

"OMG! OMG! OMG! I can't *meet* him."

"But you're his biggest fan. You came to see him, didn't you?"

"See him? Yes. Meet him? Nuh-uh."

"But—"

"Look, Frost. Sometimes I don't make sense, all right?"

Duly noted.

Aubrey might be Angelo's number one fan, but since she was practically petrified at the thought of meeting him, we skirted the edge of the ballroom, snacking and drinking and mingling.

"I mean, I've been watching him play since I was a *baby*," she said.

"I don't think I'd tell him that if I were you."

"Are you sure meeting him would be a good idea?"

"Why wouldn't it be a good idea?"

She looked down at her skirt where her fingers fidgeted with a thin layer of fabric. "Well, they say never meet your heroes, but also, well…you know."

"No, I don't know."

Her eyes locked with mine. "Don't make me say it, Frost."

"Out with it, Longfellow."

She titled her head to one side, the universal pose for "I know you're not going to make me say it."

"Yes, I am because I don't know what you're talking about."

"I'm a colossal screw up. I've had two flat tires in the past week, shown you my underwear, and tripped and bloodied my knee. Let's not forget the mayoral spaghetti incident, either."

"So?"

"So I don't have a degree! I'm working as a secretary—not even an administrative assistant—for a liquor distributor."

"People gotta drink."

"I have enough emotional baggage to sink the Titanic."

"But you're in therapy."

"Everything I touch gets messed up."

I reached over and grabbed her hand. "That is not true. Look at how well you decorated the house. Those cookies were delicious. And what about getting the virus off your parents' computer a couple of weeks ago? Or how you always plant petunias for Mrs. Potts?"

"You know about that?"

"We all know about that." Her hand felt so warm in mine. "You'll finish your degree if and when you want to. And there's no plate of spaghetti here for you to drop. Your knee looks better already."

She squeezed my hand, and my heart squeezed in return. "Do you really mean all that?"

"Of course!"

"But you've been on my case since I moved in!"

I cleared my throat. "I'm sorry about that. I had some plans that fell through, and you know how I get when plans fall through."

"Kinda uptight?"

Ouch. "Yeah. Uptight."

"But what about all the complaining about the noise and wet

clothes in the dryer and milk on the counter and, oh I don't know, remembering to pay the water bill."

"Hey, now. You've paid the water bill on time four months in a row."

"How do you know?"

My turn to grin. "Because we've still got water."

"I think I could get used to this kinder and gentler Cole Frost who doesn't yell across the mall at me."

I could definitely get used to this playful and poised Aubrey Longfellow, but I didn't dare say that out loud. I held out my hand. "Say, would you like to dance?"

"Heck, yeah, I would! But first I need to powder my nose."

The ancient euphemism was weird coming out of her young lips, but I didn't say anything. Instead, I flexed my now empty hand while enjoying the view as she walked away.

9

Aubrey

I ran my fingers across the palm of my hand as I headed to the restroom. Cole Frost had held my hand. Even stranger, I had liked it. Maybe Christmas really was a time for miracles.

Get real. What you really liked was how he had your back. He assured you that you weren't a screw up.

Once I'd handled my business, I stopped in the lounge area just inside the restroom and reapplied my lipstick. I turned in front of the mirror to make sure I didn't have part of my skirt in my underwear. After flat tires and a jury summons, I didn't want to add *mooning all of Cole's fancy coworkers* to my list of mishaps.

"Say, you're Cole Frost's date, aren't you?"

I looked over to see a stunning brunette. She was taller than me and almost willowy.

"I am."

She leaned forward to apply more lipstick. "I'm so glad he's found someone."

I put two and two together and came up with six. "You must be Deidre."

"The one and only."

The diamond of her engagement ring winked, and I did some more addition. It hadn't been *that* long ago since she dumped Cole. She was moving fast.

"You know, he really is a great guy, but he's just so…boring."

My hackles rose. "He's not boring."

She kinda rolled her eyes. "He has to have a plan for *everything*. I swear he had our life thought out all the way to the matching rocking chairs in a Florida condo."

That didn't sound half bad.

"And he was already talking about children."

My biological clock reminded me of all of those adorable babies in the line to see Santa.

She took out her compact and applied more powder. "We weren't even married, and there he was, talking about a house and a good school district."

"A lot of women would love to find a man who's not afraid of commitment," I said softly.

"Well, you are welcome to him," she said with the indulgent smile of a woman who'd traded up. Or thought she had.

My hands clenched into fists. I had the irrational urge to punch her into next week.

Wait. She thought Cole and I were an item.

Of course, she thinks the two of you are an item. You're at a company Christmas party together.

Well, then.

The corners of my lips turned up in a smile that had to be Grinchian. "I'm so glad you dumped him. Boring? Not with me. And the sex? My toes are curling just thinking about later tonight. Maybe we'll leave early."

Her jaw dropped, and I twirled on my heel to exit.

I didn't even feel as though I were lying because just thinking about his proximity on the love seat the other night made my heart race. Then there was the fact my hand still felt warm and tingly at the memory of his touch.

Stop it, Aubrey.

So the two of you seem to have a little chemistry. He is still Mr. Successful McPlanny Pants and you are still Little Miss Dreamy von Screw Things Up.

As I entered the ballroom, I almost collided with him, and my hands came up to his chest to steady myself. It was a nice chest, a very nice chest.

"Bro, you're under the mistletoe," a guy said, clapping Cole's shoulder as he walked by.

We both looked up. Sure, enough, there was a huge ball of mistletoe, like the kind you might find in real life at the top of a tree.

"Oh, hi, Cole," Deidre said from behind me. I could hear a new interest in her voice.

So I reached forward and brushed his lips with mine.

I went into the kiss with a thought of "Look at what you're missing, Deidre," but soon lost myself in him. His soft, surprised lips. His aftershave. Him.

I deepened the kiss, and he met me hungrily. I could tell the moment when he remembered he was at a company Christmas party, though, because he gave a little sigh of regret and stepped back, his hands now on my bare shoulders.

"Well, I see you've moved on," Deidre said with a sniff.

His eyes never left mine even as he answered her, "Sure did."

I grinned, and he mouthed the words, "Thank you," but the bell in my clutch didn't ring.

Of course not.

That was not an unselfish act.

No, based on the tingle of my lips and the butterflies in my stomach, I'd definitely had an ulterior motive for that kiss.

Angst squeezed my heart. Falling for Cole would be a colossally stupid mistake, even by my standards. One, we were still opposites. Two, I still had to live with him. Three, my brother would kill him, even if the eventual break up was my fault.

But what if you didn't break up?

Yeah, right. Because my track record had been so stellar.

I touched my tingly lips. Might as well savor that kiss since it was two-in-one: first and last.

10

Cole

"*I* think I need a drink." And possibly a cigarette after that kiss.

I should be kicking myself for such a public display of affection at a work function, but I couldn't seem to wipe the smile off my face.

Aubrey had kissed me.

Even better, she'd kissed me in front of Deidre, who was now frowning in my direction as if she were reconsidering out relationship.

Too late, Deidre.

"Did you know?" I asked Aubrey as we strolled over to the open bar.

"Did I know what?"

"That that woman was Deidre."

"Oh, yeah. She introduced herself while we were fixing our makeup and told me she was glad you'd found someone new."

My heart lurched a little. It might've been a pity kiss.

No, there was no faking how it had felt, and she was the one who'd instigated the kiss.

"And you didn't tell her you were only here as a favor to me?"

Aubrey chuckled. "Oh, no. Something about her rubbed me the

wrong way. I decided to let her think whatever she was going to think. That's what she gets for upending your plans."

Those old plans were happily upended. My brain was hastily making new plans, better plans.

I took Aubrey's hand in mine. "Well, I appreciate that. Being dumped by a woman you proposed to is quite the blow to a man's ego."

She squeezed my hand, and we took one step closer to the front of the line. "Mama told me when I first started dating that the only relationship that would work would be the last one. Any broken relationship before that was just a learning experience."

"Or a dodged bullet."

"That too. I should've paid more attention to her last time. I wish I'd dodged that bullet, and I think I've hit my lifetime quota on learning experiences," she said with a shudder.

"Oh, no. You're not going to beat yourself up over that," I said as we finally approached the bartender and placed our orders. I got a bourbon, neat. Aubrey squealed with delight at the sight of sparkling, so I got her a flute full of bubbles.

My heart started making plans for New Year's Eve. I told it to chill.

"Thank you again for coming tonight on such short notice," I said as we stood at one of the tall tables on the periphery of the room. The band was taking a break, so we could hear each other talk for the moment.

"Are you kidding? An excuse to dress up and get fancy food and," she lifted her champagne flute, "Free bubbles? It has been no hardship, let me assure you."

But was the kiss a hardship?

It was on the tip of my tongue to ask, but I didn't. In fact, now I didn't know what to say.

We took alternating sips in a suddenly uncomfortable silence.

"Aubrey, can I—" I said just as she was saying, "Cole, could we—"

"You first," she said.

"No, ladies first, I insist."

She hesitated, and I saw my mistake. She didn't want to put herself out there and get rejected. I didn't either.

And maybe both of us were too soon out of failed relationships to contemplate a new one, but…

Her eyes grew wide. "Oh, my gosh. Ezekiel Angelo is walking this way!"

11

Aubrey

---

*E*zekiel Angelo was *standing* in front of me. Ezekiel Angelo was standing in *front* of me. Ezekiel Angelo was standing in front of *me.*

My mouth went dry. Bad enough that my heart was still beating ninety to nothing from all of the nice things Cole had said to me. Now he was shaking hands with Ezekiel Angelo.

Somehow Cole Frost had grown up from a shy, lanky boy into a confident man.

"Ezekiel, this is my date, Aubrey."

And then my favorite basketball player ever was leaning down to shake hands. His engulfed mine. And he flashed me that wide smile. The sparkle in his eyes that matched the sparkle of the huge diamond solitaire in his right ear. "Aubrey, it's so nice to meet you. How did a nerd like Frost manage to snag a beautiful woman like you?"

To my side I heard Cole say, "Hey, now!"

I needed to speak, but I couldn't make the words. I needed to make the words. If my heart beat any faster, they would have to search the hotel for one of those defibrillators they had around here for emergencies.

And this was shaping up to be an emergency.

"Huge fan of yours, Mr. Angelo," I finally managed.

"Mr. Angelo? Aw, that's my granddaddy. You can call me Zeke. What did I do to make such a big fan out of you?"

"2010 Championship. Game Two. You made thirty-four points shooting at just over fifty percent. Five rebounds. Nine assists. Three steals."

In my periphery, Cole's jaw dropped. Even Ezekiel Angelo's smile faded. "Wow. You know your stuff. You play a little ball?"

I shrugged. "A little."

"She was All-State," Cole said.

I shot him a dirty look. What did my being All-State in high school have to do with Ezekiel Angelo's stats?

I opened my mouth to say I'd played some college basketball too, but then clamped my lips shut.

That was before I flunked out of school. I definitely didn't want to take that trip down memory lane.

Ezekiel leaned back and started counting his people. "I was going to ask you to dance but forget about that. I think we need ourselves a pick-up game. Y'all can have Shorty and Metcalf on your team. Come on!"

"Uh, where are we going?" Cole asked as we followed Ezekiel and his entourage. Cole was moving at a trot, and I was practically sprinting to keep up.

Ezekiel's grin spread slowly. "There's a court on this roof."

An employee at the elevator bank tried to tell Ezekiel that the court was now closed, but he talked the man into not only allowing us access, but he also convinced him to turn on the lights upstairs.

I had not played a serious game of basketball in well over seven years when my college career ended unceremoniously after I tore a ligament. I'd played a little here and there for fun but hadn't done anything too strenuous.

Something told me that Ezekiel Angelo, for all of the crazy things he'd done, was never not serious about basketball. He was already shrugging off his suit coat and handing it to a friend. Cole loosened his tie, but he looked rather green around the gills. I used to play with him and my brother when we were kids. A brilliant tactician, Cole could whip you at a game of HORSE. Start throwing elbows in a game of one-on-one, though, and he wanted to start calling fouls as if it were a real game. He was not, I assure you, ready for this.

"Hey, Zeke," I said, digging deep for a bravado I didn't really feel. "How about you and me play this game, one-on-one?"

He took in my dress and laughed. "You serious?"

"Deadly so."

"All right, all right."

"What are you doing?" Cole somehow managed to whisper between his teeth.

"Saving you from embarrassment," I said as I sat down on a nearby bench and leaned over to unbuckle my strappy heels.

"But what if you lose?"

I shot him a look. "Of course I'm going to lose! I'm an amateur who's over two feet shorter than he is. But nothing's on the line for me except my pride. All I have to do is keep up."

"But Aubrey, what if you get hurt?"

I laughed as I reached for the other buckle. "I'm not going to get hurt. I can throw elbows with the best of them. Here. Hold my shoes and purse."

"This is nuts," he muttered under his breath.

I looked over my shoulder to Ezekiel. "Hey, big man. Why don't you take your shoes off, too?"

"Are you serious?"

"Yeah, I'm serious. I don't want you stepping on my feet with those expensive loafers."

He grinned and sat down to take off a pair of shoes that probably cost more than my car.

To be fair, his loafers were Italian lizard skin; my car was 2001 Corolla on its last gasp.

I stood, and Cole grabbed my arm. "Aubrey. You don't have to do this."

"Sure don't, but I want to. It's going to be fun."

And terrifying.

But one advantage of having screwed up as many things as I had was that the expectations were low. No one expected this to go well for me. No one expected much of anything to go well for me.

Eventually, I was going to surprise everyone. Tonight might even be the night.

I exhaled and rolled my head around on my shoulders then started stretching as I would have before a game.

It's all muscle memory, Aubrey. All muscle memory.

I wanted to practice with a few layups, but Angelo was already dribbling between his legs and grinning at me.

"How about ladies first?" Cole said.

"Of course." Ezekiel bounced the ball to me, hard.

I caught it, and that old adrenalin started thrumming through me. I dribbled a bit then stopped, just getting a feel for things before I advanced on only one of the best guards to ever play the game.

He easily batted the ball away from me and sunk a basket in a fade shot.

I gritted my teeth and stepped under the basket to retrieve the ball.

To be quite honest, I'd played point guard. My strength had always been figuring out who to pass the ball to. Even so, I dribbled around him and feinted left before whirling around to shoot right.

It bounced off the rim, and he and his entourage all laughed.

I reached for the ball, but he easily grabbed it above my head. His eyes met mine. He was enjoying this entirely too much, like a predator toying with his prey. It made me want to tell him to pick on someone his own size, but I'd chosen this smackdown.

He made a drive for the basket. I threw an elbow.

Swoosh.

I took the ball and dribbled out from under the net while he preened for his friends. He took his time advancing because he thought there was no way I could make a three-pointer when I couldn't make a shot under the basket.

Or could I?

I knew something Ezekiel Angelo did not know: I was what they like to call a gamer. Adrenalin was my friend. It helped me do the improbable, if not the impossible.

I got into position. He charged. That sweet adrenalin pulsed through my veins. I shot. He jumped, but it was too late to actually tip the ball.

Please, Saint Sebastian, do me this one solid, I prayed to the patron saint of basketball.

It felt as though we were all moving in slow motion as the ball sank and then…nothing but net.

Whooping and hollering, I jumped up to cheer but then felt a stabbing pain in my heel.

Ezekiel Angelo had already retrieved the ball and quickly sunk another shot, while I sat on my ass looking at my bleeding heel.

The Not So Nice List had struck yet again.

"Aubrey!" Cole was across the rooftop court in a half second, looking at my heel even while I stared at the blood in a kind of shock. Then the nausea came, so I looked away as the world turned a little fuzzy.

Breathe, Aubrey, Breathe. You will not embarrass Cole by passing out. You will not —

"It's glass," he said. "Anyone got a towel?"

The guys shrugged, and Cole began to unbutton his dress shirt.

"Cole, this is hardly the time," I said, even though my voice sounded disconnected from my body. I didn't like the sight of blood, especially not my own. It wasn't a great attribute for an athlete, really. I once had to take a break during a very important game because I got elbowed in the nose.

Breathe through it, Aubrey. You can't pass out in front of Ezekiel Angelo. You just can't.

Cole handed me his dress shirt and drew a white undershirt over his head. Under other circumstances, I would've appreciated the scenery because Cole, it turned out, was no stranger to the gym. And that was my last observation before the world narrowed, blackening around the edges.

12

Cole

"*E*zekiel, could I borrow your limo?"

"Sure, Frostman. Anything you want. I sure didn't mean for your lady to get hurt." For all the grief the man was giving me over his contract, his concern for Aubrey was real. She'd been right, of course. All she had to do was show some pluck, as she had with that three-pointer out of nowhere, and she'd won his eternal admiration.

I hadn't gotten over the surprise of her perfect shot before having to move on to the shock of her foot, but I needed to be in efficiency mode right now. Later I could be shocked.

Ezekiel was still looking at me expectantly.

I scooped Aubrey up into my arms. "It's not your fault. Some jackass left his beer bottle up here to get broken."

I knew they shouldn't have been playing barefoot. But I also didn't see how Aubrey was supposed to play in her heels. Besides, she'd seemed so sure of herself.

"Where am I?" she asked as we entered the elevator.

"You are at the Hotel Madison where you stepped on a piece of beer bottle, but I have wrapped up your foot, and we're off to get stitches."

"What was the final score?" she asked.

"The heck does that matter?"

"Six to three," Ezekiel said from behind me. "But I'm pretty sure you were about to stage a comeback and whip my ass."

"Damn right I was," she said.

Ezekiel gave a low chuckle, and a bell dinged to announce we'd blessedly made a straight shot down to the ground floor.

People's heads turned as we walked through the lobby. The limo was already waiting. When Ezekiel Angelo asked for something, he got it. Immediately.

He leaned over the open door as I shifted Aubrey into a seat and picked up her heel to apply pressure to her wound. "I told the driver to take you to a doctor I know. We can't have a star basketball player waiting in the emergency room, now can we?"

"Thank you," I said.

"You're the best, Zeke!" Aubrey said, her glazed eyes incongruent with her cheerful tone.

Grinning at her use of his nickname, he shut the door and off we went.

"Sorry about that," Aubrey said as she leaned her head back against the seat and closed her eyes.

"No, I'm the one who's sorry," I said. I had that hollow feeling in my throat and stomach, the one you got when someone else was hurting and you were powerless to stop it. "It's my fault. I should've never let you do that."

"Let me," she said with a snort. "Frost, I would've thought that you of all people would know that I'm going to do what I'm going to do."

True, and she wasn't the annoying kid sister always upending Zach's and my plans, not anymore. "Does it hurt really bad?"

"Throbs like a sonuvabitch, but I've had cramps that were worse," she said. "Just as long as I don't look at it, I'll be fine."

Tough as she was, she'd always been this way about anything more than a minor cut or scrape. Once Zach and I had been wrestling in the front yard at Ms Ruth's house. He'd accidentally busted my lip, but Aubrey had been the one to faint dead away.

I still had no idea how she'd made it through so many years of playing basketball. Bruises and pain didn't phase her, but she always needed to take a moment at the sight of blood. She'd missed almost the entire second half of a regional playoff game in high school when someone busted her nose, but when she did come back to the court, she sunk the winning shot.

How could she have forgotten how clutch she was at basketball? Did it have something to do with tearing her ACL while playing in college? Try as she might, that was an injury she never quite overcame.

She sat up suddenly. "Where are my purse and shoes?"

"Right here," I said, holding them both up. One of Ezekiel's entourage had placed them in the limo beside us.

She slumped back against the seat.

I went back to applying pressure to her heel. "I wish I could take this pain for you."

"Don't be silly. Sorry I made you cut out early from the party. Hope I didn't embarrass you in front of Ezekiel Angelo."

"Are you kidding? You may have given me some leverage. How did you even make that three? Have you been playing on the sly?"

"Nope. That was divine intervention." She opened her eyes but looked steadfastly forward and away from her foot clad in my undershirt, which was now soaked in blood. It was probably about to drip on the carpet of the limo.

"I said a little prayer," she added in a small voice.

"I'm definitely a believer in the power of prayer now."

"Hey! What are you saying about my basketball abilities?" She slapped my arm as the limo made a sharp turn and came to a stop.

"I'm just saying!"

She gave me a dirty glare but crooked her arm around my neck as I slid her across the seat. The chauffeur opened the door and helped hoist her into my arms.

"Where are we?"

"We're at the address Mr. Angelo told me to put into my GPS," he said.

The mystery address was a huge brick home that was four stories tall and goodness only knew how many square feet. We were parked in front of four garages, and one of the doors was coming up.

"Come on in," said a man, hunched over with age. He'd clearly been expecting us. He didn't wait to make sure we were following before turning around to lead the way. We passed a seventy-eight Sting-Ray Corvette to the right and a Ducati motorcycle to the left. Then we went up some steps and into the world's largest mud room.

"This is incredible," Aubrey mumbled.

We stopped at a table with a bench in what had to be the breakfast nook. The kitchen beyond was commercial grade with granite counters and all kinds of cabinets. The doctor sat down a small plastic tub full of liquid. "Put your foot in there and then tell me more about what happened."

Aubrey kept her eyes on the doctor and told him the story as I unwrapped her foot and gently placed it in warm water that immediately went pink.

"Huh," the doctor said after she was finished. "You really got a three off Zeke?"

She grinned, and a part of me relaxed in relief.

"I sure did, and it's going to be worth the stitches."

The doctor chuckled. "We'll see about that. You let that foot soak for just a few minutes in that antiseptic solution, and we'll see how brave you really are. I've got my kit, but I'm going to need more light and a better pair of glasses. I'm used to dealing with bigger feet than yours!" He walked out of the room to gather his supplies.

"Sweet of him, but that's a size nine and a half down there," Aubrey quipped. She seemed to be studying the kitchen to keep from thinking about her foot.

"You know what they say about women with big feet," I said, raising my eyebrows.

Her eyes turned to me, and she scowled. "No. What is that?"

"It was a joke! I was just trying to lighten the mood."

"I can talk about my big feet, but you have to pretend that they are dainty, thank you very much."

"They are dainty. I like the blue nail polish."

She made the mistake of looking down and immediately looked back up with a nauseated grimace on her face.

I struggled to think of something to get her mind off the injury, but I couldn't think of anything. Blessedly, the doctor returned about that time and began his ministrations.

"Think you could lie down on the table?"

"Uh, I guess?"

"Help her up, son. This would be easier in the emergency room, but you would've had to have waited a lot longer for it. And I am quite the seamstress, if I do say so myself."

I hoisted Aubrey up on the table, and she lay down, trying to be demure with her short little skirt with one leg in the air. I draped my suit coat over her skirt, even though the doctor and I were too intent on her foot to be anything less than gentlemen.

With a light on his head and stronger glasses, he checked for shards of glass and bits of asphalt before declaring, "Clean cut, not even jagged. If you're gonna cut yourself, that's the way you wanna do it."

"Yay me?" Aubrey said from the table, her hands clenched at her sides.

"A little numbing agent," he said as he inserted a hypodermic. Then he got out his needle and thread.

I had to look away this time. I was holding up Aubrey's leg with my left arm so I reached to hold her hand with my right. She squeezed tightly.

Our eyes met. I moved ever so slightly to block her view of her own foot. I didn't like how pale her face was or how she'd pressed her lips into a thin line of concentration.

"Five of the prettiest stitches I've ever made," the doctor finally said before rattling off a list of care instructions and making Aubrey promise to go to her doctor the very next day.

"Say, I didn't catch your name," she said.

"Dr. Rosenberg, at your service," he said with a little bow.

"Thank you, Dr. Rosenberg."

"A fine thanks for me will be a promise to wear proper footwear in all future basketball games."

Aubrey grinned. "I can promise you that."

I scooped her up once more, and the good doctor led us out to where the limo was waiting. We rode in silence until Aubrey looked up from her phone. "Uh, that's Dr. Josiah Rosenberg. He's only a world-famous podiatrist."

I had to laugh. "Of course he was. And now you have pretty stitches for your dainty feet."

13

Aubrey

After one last ride in Ezekiel Angelo's limo, Cole carried me in the house in spite of my protests that he was going to throw his back out if he kept carting my carcass around.

"It's the least I can do," he said.

Now that my foot was fixed up and properly bandaged, I'd become very aware of the fact that he was running around with his dress shirt open. His chest was warm against my arm, and he somehow managed to still smell good in spite of all of the carrying.

He gently placed me on the love seat and plopped down on my left. Then he popped right back up and pulled the coffee table closer, grabbed a pillow, and guided my foot to the pillow. Once my injury was elevated, he sat back down again.

"You're good in a crisis, Frost."

"You're good with people, Longfellow."

We let those compliments sit in the air between us. We'd hardly spoken for the first six months I'd moved in, and, by then, we'd settled into a prickly truce. Of course, now I knew his gloomy disposition was probably due to having had his heart stomped by a woman who couldn't appreciate his finer points.

To be fair, I hadn't been able to appreciate his finer points, either.

"How can I be this tired and still not be able to fall asleep?" he asked.

"Adrenalin rush," I said. "It's kinda like trying to come down after a big game. But with stitches!"

"Oh, fun," he said. "How do we get over that?"

"Chamomile tea or—"

Sex.

He was already up and moving before I could put words to my second suggestion, which was good for many reasons. I couldn't think of any, but there had to be reasons. After a few minutes, he brought a mug of tea and a bottle of over-the-counter painkillers.

"Deidre is an idiot," I said with a sigh as I warmed my hands on the mug of tea.

He chuckled. "Thank you for that assessment."

"Seriously, you're going to make someone a mighty fine wife one day."

He laughed out loud this time. "I'll take that as a compliment."

"I meant it as one. Gender rules are stupid."

We sipped in silence for a while before he asked, "So you don't want children?"

"When did I say that? I actually would like very much to have children and be a mother, but I'm looking for the kind of guy who'll split the chores right down the middle."

"That's fair," he said.

Huh. Based on Deidre's description of Cole's plans, I'd would've guessed he wanted a little woman to cook for him— especially after the way his eyes lit up the other day when he came home to see me wearing an apron while holding a tray of cookies.

"And I think guys should be able to stay at home if they want to," I said slowly.

"Me, too." He turned those hazel eyes on me, and I was in danger of getting lost in them. "If a family can somehow afford to be one-income, why does it matter which parent stays home?"

Be still my heart.

We continued to drink our tea, and the chamomile slowly worked its magic. My eyelids were getting heavy when Cole asked, "And what about you? Thinking of making a career in liquor distribution?"

I spewed a little of my tea and went into a coughing jag that had him pounding on my back. I looked him in the eye and deadpanned, "It's been my lifelong dream, Frost."

He chuckled. "Seriously, Longfellow, why are you still at that job?"

I took in a deep, ragged breath. "Because I'm trying to prove to my parents that I am a responsible adult. I'm tired of hearing, 'Why can't you be more like your brother? Zach is already a Vice-President of Very Important Things.' Step one was to keep a job for at least a year, preferably so I can get a new job lined up before leaving this one."

"And step two?"

"To make the new job a better job?"

"But what kind of job would make you happy?"

I snorted. "All jobs are just work."

We sat and sipped in silence until he heaved a sigh. "I know I overreacted in the mall the other day—"

"D'ya think?"

"But it just didn't seem like something you'd want to be doing, sitting on Santa's lap like a sexpot. Your job certainly didn't look like what you were describing to your mom last week."

I sighed deeply. "It wasn't. It isn't."

There. You admitted it.

I played with a layer of my tulle skirt. I still couldn't believe I'd played rooftop basketball with an NBA player while wearing a Christmas dress.

Although having to get stitches in my heel felt very much in keeping with my life in general and the spirit of the Not So Naughty list in particular.

"The truth is, my boss is an utter horndog, and my job is miserable."

"I knew it!" Cole looked as though he wanted to punch someone. I had some suggestions. "Why don't you quit?"

I stared at him.

"Oh, wanting to prove you can keep a job. Got it."

"That, and I'm supposed to be up for a promotion that would transfer me to a different part of the warehouse. More money *and* I would get away from Isaac."

"I'll keep my fingers crossed."

"It's supposed to be a done deal."

"Even better," he said.

We sat in silence, and his eyes closed.

How had I never noticed before that Cole Frost was devastatingly handsome, especially now with hints of a five o'clock shadow? Behind those glasses, he hid long, dark eyelashes that any woman would kill for.

Or maybe you're feeling soft toward him because he carried you around like a knight carrying a damsel in distress.

Maybe.

Or maybe I liked the fact that he would apologize for yelling, that he would stand back and let me play one-on-one with an NBA legend who was also his client, and that he wasn't dedicated to a June Cleaver aesthetic as I'd so foolishly assumed.

His eyelids fluttered open, and I learned a new definition for bedroom eyes.

"I think I'd better get you to bed before I fall asleep," he said in a low rumbling voice.

I swallowed hard. Did I dare ask him to spend the night with me? Everything on my body was working fine—humming even—except for a thin line of stitches on my heel, thank you very much.

He picked me up, and I made a yelping noise.

"Are you okay? Did I hurt you?"

"No, no." Quite the opposite.

He carried me down the hall and somehow managed to get me

through the doorway without hitting any part of me on the frame. "Do you have a plan for getting out of that dress?"

A plan came to mind, but it wasn't a good plan—for several of those reasons I hadn't been able to think of earlier. "Could you just unzip me and grab a tee shirt from that drawer?"

He sat me down on the bed and did as he was asked, and I couldn't help but wonder what it would be like to have him unzip my dress under other circumstances.

That little muscle in his jaw twitched, and I wondered if he might be imagining the same thing.

"Right. Anything else I can get you?" he asked in a businesslike tone.

A kiss, a caress, a refresher on what sex ought to be like?

But I couldn't form the words. He was still…Cole: a nuisance, my brother's best friend, and the man with a million plans. He was always thinking ahead. If it hadn't been for him, I would've ended up sleeping in this uncomfortable dress. It was awfully hard to unzip unless I was standing, and that was something I couldn't do very well at the moment.

I, on the other hand, was still me: a screw up, the annoying little sister who tagged along where she shouldn't go, and a woman with an uncanny ability to upend plans, even her own.

He leaned toward me. I swayed toward him. For half a second, I thought he was going to kiss me. At the last minute, however, he straightened up and gave me a tired but genuine smile. "Good night, Longfellow."

"Night, Frost," I said.

There's no way Cole Frost would ever make plans that included an unsophisticated woman like me.

———

THE NEXT DAY WAS A FRIDAY, SO I CALLED IN SICK. AGAIN.

Isaac was apoplectic, but I didn't know how I was even going to drive into work the way my foot was bandaged up. Besides, I'd promised Dr. Rosenberg that I'd see my doctor.

I didn't expect Cole to take the day off, too.

"Don't you have to go to work?" I asked.

"Technically, I'm working from home," he said. "I can finish my reports and hopefully figure out this contract. Then I'll walk over to the office to make sure everything's okay before the holiday break."

I had intended to make him Nuts and Bolts, but I didn't see how I was going to do that when I wasn't even supposed to be standing up. I would have to think of something else selfless to do. Something that didn't require…walking.

"Besides," he said, "you need someone to get you to the doctor so you can get crutches."

Here he was doing things for me when I needed to be doing stuff for him. Why did I have to be so clumsy as to step on that glass?

Because that's who you are. If you can find a way to screw something up, you will.

That wasn't being completely fair to myself. Even if the whole Not So Nice List thing wasn't real, there's no accounting in this world for eccentric professional athletes. Or for idiots who don't pick up after themselves.

Mainly the idiots who don't pick up after themselves.

Cole held out his arms to me, and a part of me wanted to snuggle up beside him. He frowned when I didn't automatically lean his way. "Last time, I promise. Then we'll outfit you out with crutches."

I felt bad that he misunderstood my reluctance. Oh, I wanted to be in his arms, but I wanted to be there for an entirely different reason. I smiled, saying, "I'm just worried about your back."

"Don't be," he said as he scooped me up.

In the light of day, it felt weird to let him carry me around. My arms couldn't decide how tightly or how loosely to wrap around his neck. He'd showered and smelled as fresh as a daisy. I'd done the quickest of sink baths and didn't want to think too much about my own status.

He'd wanted to help me get ready, but I'd convinced him I could throw a knit dress over my head and hobble into the bathroom long enough to brush my hair and teeth.

Ever competent, he got me to the doctor and the pharmacy all in the comfort of his Lexus, which was a much nicer car than mine. He insisted on buying lunch for us both and then set me up in the living room to watch television with my foot propped up.

"Do you need me to turn down the volume?" I asked.

"No, I have headphones," he said as he took a seat at the dining room table.

"Want me to look at the contract?"

"What?"

"You said there was something about the contract that Ezekiel Angelo didn't like, and I am his number one fan—"

"Ha! I think he's your number one fan now. He texted this morning to check on you."

"Really?" My heart contracted. "That's sweet." I reached out an arm for the contract.

Cole tilted his head to one side, looking at me as if I were a little nutty. "You *want* to read a contract?"

I shrugged. "What else do I have to do?"

14

Cole

---

*K*eeping my eyes on my laptop and away from Aubrey was a chore. I read the digital copy of the contract on my laptop while she read the hard copy. She looked utterly adorable with her lips pursed and her brow furrowed in deep concentration.

The silence between us was rather companionable and a pleasant surprise. Of course, it was also full of electricity—at least on my part. I'd wanted so badly to kiss her last night, but I couldn't bring myself to ask, knowing that her foot had to be hurting her.

I'd thought I wanted someone like Deidre. She was professional, poised, and always knew what she wanted and where she was going. Now I had to admit that Aubrey's propensity to do the unexpected—like play one-on-one in a Christmas dress —was...hot.

Though I felt terrible that she'd hurt herself doing something for me.

Ezekiel Angelo must've felt a little remorse, too, because he'd sent a huge bouquet of flowers for her.

Too bad he hadn't felt enough remorse to sign the damn contract. I was behind on all of my reports, but I needed to figure

71

the contract out first because it was my largest potential commission.

My eyes glazed over. I'd read all of these boring words so many times before.

"A-ha!"

I turned to see a triumphant Aubrey.

"You don't have a rider in the contract specifying that the players will be announced in alphabetical order."

"Huh?"

She sighed in exasperation. Half of my confusion was from the words coming out of her mouth, and the other half was from how a woman could still look so sexy in such a shapeless dress while her hair was being held up in a bun by a friggin' pencil. I had so many questions.

"Cole. How much do you know about basketball and the Atlanta Firebirds?"

"Not much. More of a baseball guy, really."

She grabbed her crutches and hobbled over to the table to sit by me. "Look, the 2010 Championship almost didn't happen because Ezekiel couldn't get along with Jonah Wheaton. Jonah accused him of being selfish with the ball. Ezekiel shot back that he had to be selfish because Jonah couldn't make a basket in pressure situations. It was a whole thing."

"But what does that have to do with the players being announced in alphabetical order?"

"I don't know for sure, but I noticed that from that point on, they always announced the players alphabetically. Ezekiel would come out first and the whole team would be between him and Jonah. It's like a literal buffer."

It couldn't be that easy, could it? Well, it didn't make any less sense than the Beethoven request. I picked up my phone to call Luis who sighed with relief when I made the suggestion. Our long national nightmare was over!

I leaped across the table and kissed Aubrey full on the lips. "You are a genius!"

Somewhere beyond me a sleigh bell rang, but I didn't think much of it. Besides, I was already stuffing papers in my satchel and shutting my laptop. "I'm going to run to the office and take care of all of this and make sure that everyone is up to speed before the break. When I get back, though? Champagne. Or chocolate. Anything you want on me!"

It was only when I was halfway to work, whistling all the way, that I realized I had kissed her again. My stomach tied and untied a hundred knots, but I couldn't worry about what that kiss meant —if anything—right now.

I would take care of business, and then I would worry about what I would say to Aubrey when I got home.

15

Aubrey

Sometimes I thought I could still feel the tingle on my lips from the kiss Cole had given me a week ago. That night he'd brought the champagne as promised, but he'd also come back reserved. We'd been tiptoeing around each other with extraordinary politeness. This new distance was more excruciating than our previous situation. Things were so much easier when I thought he was a stick in the mud.

At least my explanation of his contract woes had made the sleigh bell ring. Two down, and one to go. I hadn't thought of reading a contract as selfless, but who was I to argue with Santa?

Also, I could now walk without crutches, as long as I took it easy. My biggest problem was that I only had two days to make that blasted bell ring once more, and I was pretty sure that meant I needed to find the perfect Christmas gift for Cole.

It would have to be super big. It would have mean giving up something for myself.

I had no ideas.

Even worse, Isaac was particularly handsy as of late. I hadn't seen the blonde woman he'd interviewed since the day I took the calendar to the printer, but he kept dropping even more hints that he would like for him and me to become more than friends.

Okay, so they weren't hints. They were pretty explicit.

I grit my teeth. The promotion was supposed to come through any day now.

"Aubrey, could you come see me for a minute?" Isaac's voice came over the loudspeaker.

Oh, please let the promotion have come through. Oh, please let the promotion have come thorough. Oh, please—

When I entered Isaac's office, he was leaning against the corner of his desk, looking really proud of himself. Of course, he would try to take credit for everything even though I'd been the one to scour all of the intracompany listings. I'd filled out the applications and done the interviews and listed him as my supervisor, to which he'd frowned and said, "But why would you want to leave my department?"

After talking with the manager above him, he'd changed his tune, often dropping hints that he was going to do me a huge favor.

"Well, Aubrey, I need to talk to you about the coordinator position."

My heart sped up.

"When Genevieve comes in, I need you to get her up to speed on what we do around here."

A-ha! He had hired the blond woman to take my place. I opened my mouth to say I'd be happy to, but he kept speaking. "She's going to need to get a lay of the land since she's coming in from a textile manufacturer, but I think she'll get the hang of everything soon enough—"

The hang of answering the phone, keeping up with Isaac's calendar, and dodging his pinches? Pretty sure she didn't need me for that.

"She's going to be spending most of her time in the Long Branch office, but—"

Long Branch office? That made no sense. The promotion was supposed to send *me* to the Long Branch office. Blood rushed in my ears, drowning out Isaac's pontificating.

He hadn't. He *couldn't* have.

Finally, I blurted, "You gave her my promotion, didn't you?"

He cleared his throat and made a few other sounds that weren't quite grunts. "Well, technically, it wasn't your job yet. She did have more experience, and…"

He shrugged. He had the audacity to shrug off all of my hopes, all of the hard work I'd put into staying at this godforsaken job in an attempt to prove to my parents and my brother and yes, God help me, Cole, that I could finish what I started.

"So she gets the coordinator position, and I'm supposed to keep working for you?"

He smiled with relief. "Yes! You get it. You just don't have that much experience in liquor distribution. The big boss and I thought it would be better for you to stay in this position a little longer."

"But you want me to show her the ropes."

"Well, just the basics," he said.

"Are you going to have her dress in a skimpy dress and pose with Santa?"

"Now, Aubrey, that was all fun and games. You have such good legs that it would be a crime to hide them."

"Are you going to pinch her behind when she walks by and make jokes about your penis to her?"

"It's all just a joke, Aubrey. Why can't any of you women ever take a joke?"

A joke? My blood boiled, rage simmering so deeply inside me that I spoke before I thought. "It's sexual harassment, that's what it is, and I am through. Consider this my two weeks' notice."

And just like that his expression contorted into anger. "You can't leave me in the lurch like this! You know we've got shipments going everywhere for Christmas and then New Year's."

"In two weeks, I'm out. And I'm off for Christmas Day."

"You know what? Clear out your stuff. If you're going to leave after everything I've done for you, after giving you a job when you didn't have jackshit on your resume, then just get out. And don't have anyone call me for a reference, either."

"Don't worry. I won't."

I stalked to my desk and loaded what few personal effects I had into an old paper box.

After all that he'd done for me. He'd only hired me because he'd seen someone young and inexperienced, someone he thought he could talk into sleeping with him.

I took a few minutes to clear anything personal from the company laptop, though there wasn't much. On a whim, I downloaded a copy of all of my emails—both sent and received—to my Dropbox file.

Just in case.

By the time I got home, my anger and bravado had melted into something akin to sorrow. Now what was I going to do? I'd proven once again that I, Aubrey Longfellow, could not hold a job for longer than five months.

If Grandma hadn't left this bungalow to Zach and me, then I would've never left my parents' basement. Except for my last relationship, where I spent entirely too much time living in what I was pretty sure was a commune.

How was I ever supposed to get a decent job if I had no degree? And if I couldn't trust myself to pick out a boss who wouldn't harass me?

I'd said it once. I'd probably say it again: I was the hottest of messes.

The house.

The house was all I had, so it was the only thing I had to give Cole. I mean, not give. But I could finally agree to sell the house to him like my brother wanted me to do. Zach and I could split the difference, and I would move in with my parents while I decided what to do next.

It was the logical thing to do. The responsible thing. The sort of thing Cole would do if he were ever in my shoes, which I couldn't even imagine.

I leaned forward and slapped my forehead on the kitchen table.

I didn't want to leave this house. I loved it. I had always loved it. The fact that Grandma had given me this small piece of independence had kept me going through that crappy job.

Unfortunately, I needed the capital from the house if I wanted to finish my college degree, and I was going to need that degree if I wanted to find a job I could tolerate.

Maybe.

Probably.

Best not to take any chances.

At least I would know the house would be in good hands with Cole. He would always remember to change the air filters. He'd paint the exterior on a regular basis and do a better job of keeping weeds out of the lawn. Yeah, the house would be better off in his hands anyway.

I might as well walk around the house and say goodbye to all of its nooks and crannies. The elf said I had to do something selfless. Maybe I wasn't being entirely selfless because I was going to sell the house for money, but it sure as heck was going to hurt.

Oh, screw the elf. Screw the Not So Naughty list. Luck didn't really exist.

This was all just Aubrey being Aubrey.

16

Cole

J was beginning to worry about Aubrey.

If I didn't know any better, I'd think she'd been avoiding me.

Yeah, because you've been avoiding her.

Okay, sure. I'd been avoiding her. I still didn't know what to say to her. I knew what I wanted to say, "Hey, Aubrey, let's try dating. Maybe if it goes well, we can get married and have at least two kids!"

But that wasn't the thing you said to your best friend's sister— at least that's what I'd heard. Besides, Deidre had visibly recoiled when I laid out my plans for us. What if Aubrey did the same?

Well, it's Christmas Eve, so you're going to have to do something.

Three o'clock on Christmas Eve, to be exact. I could've left the office at noon, but I still had no idea what to get Aubrey for Christmas. I only knew I had to get her something special. Jewelry? Too intimate. Rhinestones for her crutches? Too temporary. She hardly used them anymore.

I mean, I had an autograph from Ezekiel Angelo. I'd secured that once I got the contract ironed out to his specifications, but that wouldn't be such a big deal now that she'd played one-on-one with the guy and ridden in his limousine. Besides, he'd signed the cards that came with her flowers, so she already had his autograph.

I packed up my satchel—including the autograph—and prepared to leave my office for the last time that year. I wasn't going to figure out a gift for Aubrey in the office, and I had to think of something.

Art supplies? She was always doing something in the basement, but I was afraid I would get the wrong kind of supplies. She experimented with so many different mediums. I guess I could get her a gift card to some art store, but that didn't feel personal.

How about gardening supplies? No, it was too cold for them at the moment, and I didn't even know if she actually liked planting the petunias or if she just did it because Mrs. Potts enjoyed them.

There was so much about Aubrey Longfellow that I somehow still didn't know.

But I wanted so desperately to find out.

I grabbed my satchel and headed out the door. Should I take her out to dinner? No, that was an excuse to take her on a date without having to ask her on a date because I was afraid that she'd say no if I did. Movies? A concert?

The elevator dinged and I stepped inside with a deep sigh.

Wait. There it is.

On the wall, someone had taken a picture of a box of kittens. They were free to a good home, and along the fringe at the bottom of the page were numbers you could tear off and call.

The first month we'd lived together, she bugged the snot out of me to get a kitten. I'd originally said no because Deidre was allergic, but I also didn't want to have to clean up the litter. At the time, I'd thought Aubrey wouldn't be responsible enough to do it, but now I knew she was perfectly responsible enough to take care of people and pets. I'd just believed what her brother and parents had told me rather than looking for myself.

But if I got a kitten, that would require planning.

I couldn't help but smile. Planning is what I did best.

It took longer than I'd anticipated to get the kittens.

The pet store had been crazy busy with people buying last minute pet supplies. Then I'd gone to the house of one of my coworkers, where I'd stood over the box of kittens unable to decide which one to get. Finally, I chose two. They were sisters, and one was a muted tortoiseshell calico while the other was solid black.

On the seat beside me they were mewing almost pitifully, which was going to ruin my surprise. But I absolutely couldn't wait to see Aubrey's face when she saw them. I opened the top of the box where they were nestled on a towel. "Look, you're going to love her, and you're only going to be in this box just a little while longer. As soon as she opens the box, then I'll get your litter and your food and everything else you need."

In response, they mewed at me. Especially, the tortoiseshell one. I could tell she was going to be trouble.

I hummed "Jingle Bells" as I juggled the box on one hip in order to close the car door. I had a bounce in my step as I climbed the stairs to the front door. Why hadn't I just told Aubrey she could get a kitten in the first place?

Of course, if I'd done that then I wouldn't have the perfect gift for her right now.

When I walked in, she was at the counter making a salad to go with the pizza she'd ordered. She wore the ugliest Christmas sweater I'd ever seen. It prominently featured a festive llama of all things.

I put down my box. "Hey, you shouldn't be standing on that foot yet."

She turned around, and I could see she'd been crying. Thank goodness I had just the thing to cheer her up.

"I'll finish the salad for you in a minute," I said, gesturing for her to take a seat at the table.

"There's enough for both of us, if you'd like."

"Even better, but first I want you to open the Christmas gift I got you."

"Oh, Cole. You didn't have to do that," she said.

"Of course, I did."

She sat down and wrung her hands. "Maybe I should wait until tomorrow."

I stared at her and stared at the box, but it did not mew. It was as though the kittens were in on it with me.

"Just open it. Please?

I'd wrapped the top and the bottom separately—always planning—so all she had to do was remove the lid.

"Oh," she said, the sound of her voice piercing my heart in a good way. "Oh. They're adorable."

She picked up the black kitten and ran her face against its soft fur.

And then she started to cry.

17

Aubrey

Cole's face blanched. Or I thought it did. It was hard to see through my tears.

"I can take them back," he said.

"No, oh please don't," I finally managed over the lump in my throat.

He had brought me kittens. He had been listening to me all along. He wasn't the stick in the mud I'd thought he was.

"These are mostly happy tears," I said.

"Mostly?"

I put the wiggly black kitten back in the box and picked up the tortoise colored one. She immediately began to purr with a force much greater than her small size. I gestured to a small box on the table. "I love the kitties. That present is for you."

He tore into the wrapping paper, the expression on his face somewhere between amusement and curiosity. He opened the box and found a key. His smile disappeared. "What does this go to?"

"Our—This house. I called Zach and told him I was willing to sell it as long as it was going to you."

The jingle bell, still in the clutch I'd tossed on an end table after the Christmas party, jingled its last.

I sighed. I was officially off the Not So Nice List. More importantly, for the first time in my life I'd seen a task through all the way to its bitter end.

"But this is your home," Cole said.

I put the kitten back in the box and wiped away tears with the heel of my hand. "I…I quit my job. I need to sell the house to have the money to go back to school. I'll move in with my parents."

"You quit your job?" His brow furrowed. I could see that it was concern now. It wasn't judgment. "What happened?"

I told him about seventy-five percent of the story. "And that's it. I'm not even sure why I'm trying again because I just keep screwing up, but I guess I have to keep trying, right? Can't wait to have Mom and Dad be on my case again, asking if I've done my homework and if I really need to go out with that boy or—"

"Stay with me."

My heart soared upward, thudding against my rib cage. Those were the words I'd wanted to hear, but was he asking me to stay as a friend or something more? "Cole, I—"

He handed me the key back and gently closed my fingers over it. "I'll keep paying rent to your brother. I can take care of the utilities until you find another job."

And my heart nosedived. He was making this offer as a friend, but there was nothing like an offer of friendship to make a girl realize she wanted something more. It would be a special kind of torture to live with Cole, knowing he'd placed me so firmly in the friend zone.

Tears spilled hot and heavy down my cheeks. "I can't let you do that. How am I ever supposed to know if I can do something on my own if I don't do this? I can't be a charity case forever, Cole."

He sat down beside me and did his best to thumb away my tears before clasping my hands in his. "You are not a charity case. You just need a break. That's all. Your grandmother left this house to both you and Zach in case anyone ever needed help. Now you do."

I crumpled at his kindness.

Too often I'd heard, 'Why can't you be more like your brother?

Why are you getting an art degree? Why'd you quit school when you got injured? Why do you date losers?'

I took a deep, shuddering breath, "But what if I fail again? I'm so tired of failing and here I am quitting another job without having—"

"Stop right there. You should've never had to put up with what you did at that liquor company. That was wrong, and I wish you'd told me about it sooner, not that I know what I could've done about it. I thought you were being a little too adventurous that day in the mall. I didn't know that he was behind the whole thing. Even so, I should've kept my mouth shut."

I sucked in a breath. "Really?"

"Really."

"You are smart and brave and very good with people. Look at the way you deciphered the contract. Heck, look at the way you interacted with Ezekiel Angelo. Or…or…look at all of your art downstairs. You have talent. There's a perfect job for you out there. You just haven't found it yet."

A perfect job. Yeah.

Now I could breathe again, at least. Reluctantly, I took my hands from his and moved over to the sink to put some distance between us. I got a glass of water and drank it best I could over the lump in my throat.

The kittens filled the silence between us with mews and soft scratches.

"Guess I'd better set up a litter box for them?" Cole asked sheepishly.

I nodded, and he left the house only to return with litter, a box, cat food, and a little bag that suspiciously jingled as if it had toys. His efficiency made me feel like a slacker.

Stop it, Aubrey! It's part of your present.

"Want some pizza?" I asked lamely once he had the kittens settled in the bathroom.

He opened his mouth as if he wanted to finish our conversation from before. "Sure."

"I think it's warm salad and cold pizza now," I said. "But it's better than nothing. I mean, I'm sorry—"

"Aubrey, for heaven's sake, please don't apologize. You're offering me a supper I didn't have to cook."

"But it's a—"

"Meal I didn't have to prepare."

"It's not much, really. The least I can do is preheat the oven and—"

He walked over and gently grabbed my upper arms. His lips had thinned in determination. "If I kiss you, will that keep you from making another apology?"

I fought the urge to melt into him. "No! I mean yes. Maybe?"

"Can we find out?" he asked in a growl.

"Please?"

Then his lips were on mine. I stood on my good tiptoe to better reach him. This kiss was different from the surprised exploration under the mistletoe or the excited smack after he figured out the contract. This kiss was distinctly unplanned and more than a little…naughty.

My Christmas sweater hit the floor. Unbuttoning his shirt was taking too long, so I just ripped it open for the last three buttons. The look of surprise on his face was worth it as was the passion in the kiss that came next.

But as I reached for his belt buckle, his hand covered mine. "Wait."

Oh. I'd gone too far again. Shame heated me up as the lack of a shirt cooled me down. "Sorry."

"Don't be sorry." His hazel eyes saw all the way to my soul. "It makes me want to kiss you again."

Hope brought a flush of warmth again. "Promise?"

18

Cole

$\mathcal{I}$t took every last bit of my will power to guide Aubrey to the couch rather than kiss her into oblivion after that saucy little comment. I put her at one end and took the other end myself. As we'd already discovered, the little sofa didn't allow for that much space between us. So I got up to pace.

"I am not going to sleep with you when we haven't even discussed our relationship status much less settled your living arrangements," I said. Then I realized she should be elevating her foot and took a pillow from the couch and picked up her dainty foot and placed it on the pillow on the coffee table.

"Don't you think I need a shirt for this conversation?" She crossed her arms over her bra. It did lovely things for her cleavage.

Snap out of it.

"No. If I don't get to have a shirt, then you don't get a shirt."

She arched an eyebrow then ran her eyes over my chest in a way that made me want to preen and blush all the same time.

"You started it," she said. "And I am more than happy to finish it."

I felt a little shudder of anticipation. I had started it by kissing her out of nowhere. So far, the night hadn't gone the way I'd wanted it to at all.

"How so?"

Oh, great. Now I was thinking out loud. I took a minute for the blood that had pooled in my crotch to hopefully make its way back up to my brain where it was sorely needed.

"The original plan was to get you the perfect gift. I settled on the kittens and then…"

"And then what?"

My eyes met hers. I couldn't tell her my whole plan. If I told her my whole plan, then she would laugh me out of the house. If I told her about the future I'd envisioned, she might run away like Deidre did.

"Come on, Cole. I know you have a plan. You always have a plan."

I looked away. "Maybe I shouldn't."

"Or maybe I'll *like* the plan."

"It's too much."

She patted the spot on the couch beside her. I walked over to the tree instead.

"It's a plan. It's not like we can't change it if we need to," she said.

Change the plan? Sacrilege.

Besides, if I told her my plan, she might think I was just putting her in Deidre's place when, in reality, Deidre had been in *her* place. I just hadn't known it at the time. All of those hopes and dreams fell into place in perfect clarity. This time Aubrey had the starring role.

"But what if I'm wrong?" I asked, even though every fiber of my being screamed, *No. This time you have it right.*

"Then you have it wrong. And you start again," she said. "Trust me, I know a few things about making mistakes."

"I will kiss you again if you keep talking bad about yourself."

"Promises, promises," she said with a sigh. After a beat, she added, "Come on, Frost, tell me about your plans."

She said it with the same kind of purr that another woman

might use in inquiring about my fantasies. The two were beginning to run together.

I took a deep breath. "Step one was to get you the perfect Christmas present."

"Well done! What was step two?"

"Figure out a way to ask you out on a date."

"Good, good. We've already been on a date."

"We have?"

"The Christmas party. We got dressed up. We ate together. We kissed. That incorporates most of the elements of a date, yes?"

She had a point.

"Okay, well, after a couple of dates I was going to ask if you would…"

"Yes?"

"Be my girlfriend."

She bit her lip to keep from laughing. It did sound silly when I said it like that, but that didn't stop my whole body from stiffening in anticipation of her answer.

"The answer is yes."

Breathe. Yes, I needed to breathe. "That was easy."

"You're a very persuasive guy when you want to be."

"Somewhere in there was going to be sex."

"Obviously."

"Then after a suitable amount of time I was going to ask you to marry me." I winced, waiting for her to laugh.

Instead, she drawled, "Let's put a pin in that one. Is that the end of the plan?"

Absolutely not. I wanted to have at least two children with her adorable spunk and whatever my best quality was. I wanted to take her on trips to Caribbean resorts and art museums, to sporting events and National Parks. I wanted to argue with her about chore charts and then have delicious make up sex. I wanted to see the woman she would become, what kind of artistic mark she would make on this world. I wanted to help her become that woman. But instead of all that, I said, "I think that's more than enough for now. What do you think?"

She studied me carefully. "I think it's a solid plan, but maybe we should wing it from this point forward."

"Wing it?"

"Yes. Wing it. As in play it by ear. As in, we have been on a date. We have kissed. I will happily be your girlfriend. Now, we are going to do a little chemistry experiment and then take it from there."

"You're sure."

She stood and hobbled over to where I stood in front of the tree. "Why wouldn't I be sure?"

"You know, I'm boring Cole. I believe someone in this room once called me a stick in the mud. And—"

"Don't talk about my boyfriend like that." She pulled me in for a kiss.

This time when she reached for my belt buckle, I didn't stop her.

After all, we had some experiments to conduct. For science.

Epilogue

One Year Later

Aubrey

I should've had the oddest sense of deja-vu on my first day of my new job, but I didn't. Now I was dressed as an elf and would be taking pictures of the kids who came to see Santa starting the next day when Santa's Wonderland officially opened. It was the perfect temporary job for a student, even if it didn't play much to my talents in graphic design.

Paying the bills came first. A career would come later when I finally graduated in the spring.

Cole had taken apart my old transcript with the precision of an academic mechanic and had guided me on what to say to the advisor in order to get as many credits as humanly possible to transfer. A few semesters and maybe summer school. That's all I needed to convert my old art major into something a little more cutting edge.

This job would help me pay a chunk of the bills. Even better, I'd sifted through my old emails and journal entries to make High

Spirits Liquor Distributors aware of several events and emails that had happened while I was employed there. They were offering me a settlement. Isaac was calling me for a reference while applying for a new job. Or he had called me before I blocked his number.

That act had been an early Christmas present to myself.

"Now, you hit this button," the wizened elf woman was saying to me.

"Ho, ho, ho. If it isn't Aubrey Longfellow!" Santa had entered the chat, or, rather, he'd entered the world of picket fences, candy canes, and cotton snow and was taking his place on the throne so we could take some promotional photos now that the mall officially closed for the day.

"Oh, it's you," I said as I recognized the *real* Santa.

"Wouldn't miss it," he said. "Sometimes I have to let one of my brothers take care of mall work, but tonight is going to be a special night."

It was a Tuesday at ten p.m. There was nothing special about Tuesdays except the occasional taco. Certainly, there was nothing special about taking promotional pictures and training, but who was I to argue with Santa?

I turned back to my elf tutor, and she guided me through a couple of shots before grudgingly declaring me ready. "At least you're ready until the kids arrive tomorrow. Then we'll see what you're made of."

Sterner stuff, sister. I was made of sterner stuff, and I wasn't likely to forget it ever again.

"Well, now. What's your name, young man?"

I took a step toward Santa, ready to gently tell whoever was there that we wouldn't officially open until the next day.

"Cole Frost," my boyfriend said even though his eyes were on mine. He was wearing candy cane boxers. I slapped a hand over my mouth to keep from giggling.

"That's a Christmas name, if I've ever heard one," Santa said. "I'd ask you to sit in my lap, but, well, how about a seat beside me instead?"

"No thanks," he said. "I think I'll kneel for this one."

He knelt and took my hand. "Aubrey Longfellow, would you do me the honor of being my wife?"

I cleared my throat. "I think a suitable amount of time has passed. Seems like a solid plan."

"So, is that a yes?"

"Yes!"

He took a silicone band, one improbably designed like a candy cane, and slipped it on my finger. "Let's leave this as a place holder until you can pick out something you'd like."

"You didn't plan for which ring I would like?" I asked as he stood and wrapped his arms around me.

"Oh, no. Buying a ring without your input would be a dangerous form of winging it."

I kissed him thoroughly.

"Careful, you two," Santa said. "You don't want to make the Not So Nice List again."

"The what?" asked Cole.

"Maybe I'll tell you sometime," I said. "After you get some pants."

He grinned. "I just thought it was only fair. Now, hopefully we'll both be thinking about candy cane underwear all the time."

"Cole Frost, you are incorrigible."

"I learned from the best."

"Oh, get a room," the elf said before turning a gnarled finger at me. "But don't be late tomorrow."

I glanced over to give Santa my thanks, but he was already gone. I took Cole's hand. "Why do I think you have something planned?"

He squeezed my hand and waggled his eyebrows. "Because I do. A lifetime of things, in fact."

"But there's a little room for me to upend those plans?" I asked with an eyebrow waggle of my own.

He looked down at me as someone who saw me just as I was and said, "I'm counting on it."

Did you enjoy The Not So Nice List? *Please consider leaving an honest review and telling your friends. Read on to learn more about source materials and other novels by Sally Kilpatrick*

Acknowledgments

All of the thanks and love to Sarah Younger, who keeps me going. If only poor Luis, the agent in this book, could take lessons from her. Thanks to all the fine folks at NYLA, especially Natanya who keeps answering my emails.

I've said it before, and I'll say it again. Take a moment to give yourself a big hug from me to you. Thank you. You keep me going, too.

Thanks to Laura Apgar for squeezing in this project and adding her editorial wisdom. I'm so glad you didn't laugh uncontrollably and tell me to go away when I first outlined the premise for you. I also promise I will try not to use the word "because" so often in the future.

Special thanks to Hailey Michna who crafted the lovely cover. I promise you that I won't have any other covers that feature Santa. Ever.

Thanks to Mom, Lisa, Ryan, and Liz for reading and commenting and helping me make this little story better. If I have somehow left you out. Please forgive me. There was a year between finishing this one and publishing it. Or a decade. Or three months. What is time?

As always, any mistakes you see—especially those about basketball, marketing, or agenting—are all my own. Or I left them for the sake of narrative flow.

I wouldn't be able to craft stories without the help of my family. Thanks, as always to Jim and Jane, Bill and Terri. Thanks to

Connor and Lorelai. This book did not happen with any help from Rocket and Blix. In fact, sometimes they made writing this book very difficult, but I thank them anyway. As always, thanks to Ryan for inspiring all of my best heroes.

Also by Sally Kilpatrick

The Happy Hour Choir

Bittersweet Creek

Better Get to Livin'

Bless Her Heart

Oh My Stars

Much Ado about Barbecue

Snowbound in Vegas (a novella)

About the Author

Sally Kilpatrick is the *USA Today* bestselling author of six novels. She has won multiple awards including the 2018 and 2019 Georgia Author of the Year, the Maggie Award of Excellence, the Booksellers' Best, and the Nancy Knight Mentorship Award. She lives in Marietta, Georgia with her dashing husband, two precocious children, and two persnickety cats. You can find her at www.sallykilpatrick.com or on Twitter as @Superwritermom.